ARI EVER AFTER

CLARKE HOPKINS

*To S, who knew that telling me I couldn't write a romance
would make me do it. Thanks, bro.*

Chapter 1

"Can I buy you a coffee?"

New thing to add to my list of pet peeves: men who refused to understand that headphones meant I didn't want to talk to them. "Excuse me?" I very obviously took out one headphone, leaning my head to the side.

"Can I buy you a coffee?" he repeated, staring directly at me.

"No, thanks." What made men think that I was interested in talking to them? I had enough of dating for the rest of my life, and I had work to do. I was busy here.

"Are you sure?" He stared at me for another second. "Because I accidentally knocked yours over."

Oh, shit. I looked down at the coffee pooling on the table. This was what I got for deciding that I could totally work from a coffee shop.

"Don't worry about it." I managed a grimace towards him, jumping up and heading to grab a stack of napkins. "I can handle it."

"But I – " he called behind me, but I was already heading back with a stack of napkins. I would fix this problem myself.

I stared down at the table for another few seconds as I wiped up the coffee. I'd thought that getting out of my apartment would make me really productive, but nope.

I was supposed to meet Raleigh at her place in an hour anyway, so there was no harm in being there early. Not that I would get any work done, but hanging out was more fun than pretending to work.

I sent her a text - *On my way early, need anything?*, then shoved my laptop back into my bag and headed out into the cold.

I turned to the right, heading towards Raleigh's apartment. She lived in the newer part of town, where there were apartments built especially for students with big windows and a doorman. Maybe if I doubled my work, I could make enough money to move into this area.

Yeah, that wasn't happening. I couldn't even manage to finish the first draft of *The Lord Who Loved Me*, and any money that I made needed to go into the Arielle Graduates Without Crippling Student Debt fund. My parents had been clear that until I got my life choices back in order, they weren't giving me a penny towards anything but my credit hours for my practical communications major.

I reached Raleigh's building and tapped in the code for the front door. I wasn't supposed to know it, but she'd added me to her guest list a long time ago. I walked up the stairs towards her apartment and pushed open the front door, looking down to see if I could see her dog anywhere. She'd rescued a Bernese Mountain Dog from the shelter a couple of years ago, and now, if anyone tried to come into the apartment unannounced, Lilyanna would let everyone know.

Lilyanna came wandering out of the kitchen towards me, and I reached down and started to pet her. "You are the best dog," I said, running my fingers through her fur. "The world's best dog. What would we do without you?"

I heard a noise and immediately looked up.

Oh no.

That wasn't Raleigh.

Mason, Raleigh's boyfriend, was standing there. Completely naked.

And I was leaning down to pet Lilyanna, putting my head right at the level of his –

Penis.

Not in clothing. Just – there. Standing right there.

I looked up and stared at him for a second, my mouth open. Oh god.

"Mason?" came Raleigh's voice from her

bedroom. "Where'd you go? I'm going to come out if you don't – "

Oh no. That was going to make things worse. Oh god.

I turned and grabbed my backpack. I threw open the front door and started to run down the hallway, away from that. The sight had already started to burn itself behind my eyes. Nope. Did not want. None of that, please.

I sprinted down the stairs. "Ari?" someone called behind me, but I wasn't stopping. If I kept running, it's like it hadn't happened.

And I definitely wasn't going to have flashbacks to the sight of Mason naked during every single dinner and movie night at Raleigh's. Nope. I would totally be able to look him in the face later.

I slowed down and walked out of the apartment, closing my eyes for a second. I could absolutely flush that image out of my face if I tried hard enough. Deep breath.

And then, in another brilliant move, I took a step with my eyes closed.

"Shit!" My foot hit ice, my legs slipping out from under me.

I went down, both of my knees smacking into the sidewalk.

God, that hurt. I picked up my hand from the ground, looking at it. Scraped. There was blood all over my palm, and I tried to brush away the dirt on it. It stung.

Okay. This was not my day. I was going to write off today. I was going to go home and make myself a nice cup of tea.

But before I could move, I heard the voice above me. "Ari?"

Oh god. And it had managed to get worse. Lucas Wolf, Mason's best friend, was standing right there, watching me. Someone had seen that. "Ari?" he asked again. "Are you okay?

"I'm fine. Totally fine." Someone had witnessed that. I deserved three cups of tea. With rum.

"You're on the ground. I don't think you're fine," he replied.

This was one of those moments where I could really use a snappy comeback. But before I could think of one, he reached down and grabbed my hands. He pulled me up, his fingers lightly around my wrist.

I took a step back, shaking my hand free from his fingers. "I just tripped. I was walking too fast coming out of the building. It's nothing."

He stared at me for a second. "Walking too fast?"

"Mason was naked. I had to get out of there before I saw any more," I said. And then I had to flush that particular mental image out of my head. "I just wanted to hang out with Raleigh, and then instead, I saw Mason naked. With Raleigh," I added, just to make that part clear.

Lucas's mouth dropped slightly. "So it's not a good time for me to take Lilyanna for a run?"

My brain decided to take this time to distract me from the fact that I'd seen my best friend's boyfriend naked by reminding me that Lucas was attractive.

Nope. I was shutting that part off too. Think about laundry. I had plenty of laundry to do at home. I cleared my throat. "You should stay far away from that apartment."

He looked down again, his eyes landing on my knee. "Ari, you're bleeding."

I looked down. Of course. I'd ripped my favorite pair of tights, and I'd torn up my knees underneath it. "It's fine. I have band-aids at home."

Not that I would actually go home. Spencer was building a robot, and there was a partially disassembled computer on the couch. She'd already threatened me with a slow and painful death if I spilled chamomile tea on any of the parts. My roommate and second best friend was a genius, but unfortunately for me, a genius of the mad scientist variety.

"I'm not letting you walk home if you're bleeding that much. Come on. We're going to my place," he said, reaching down and picking up my bag like it weighed nothing.

"I'm okay," I said, my leg immediately twinging to let me know that was a lie.

He put the bag on his shoulder and started to walk away. "We're going. It's too cold to stand outside, and you need neosporin and band-aids. Don't be ridiculous."

"But I don't need help," I started to protest, walking after him to get my backpack back.

It was useless. We were already at Lucas's car. He opened the passenger side door for me, raising an eyebrow. "After you."

Chapter 2

This was a real dilemma now. My pride wanted to walk away, but my leg didn't want to. I paused for a second, looking down at the car.

I tried to move my knee and immediately felt the scrape. My pride was going to have to take the loss here. I slid into the car, Lucas watching me. He finally shut the door behind me, then walked around and got into the driver's seat.

"I bet this car would lose in a fight against Lazzie," I said, looking around at the ridiculously clean car. There wasn't even an empty water bottle in a cupholder.

Lazzie, short for Lazarus, was a twenty-year old Toyota Corolla that Spencer and I shared custody of. We were pretty sure we could drive into a river, fish it out, and still drive it. This car would survive any natural disaster. There were a few pieces that Spencer had repaired with duct tape over time, but it could go anywhere.

"Is the reason that you drive such an old car so that no one can see the bumps on it?" He reached for the gear shift, as though to show off that he could drive stick. Goddamn it. That was another of those things that I found attractive even if I shouldn't.

"Don't insult our driving. Lazzie is going to outlast all of us. It's already old enough to vote and drink. We got it a beer last year to celebrate its twenty-first birthday," I replied.

"You bought your car a beer." He sounded like he was about to start laughing, but I shot him the nastiest look that I could manage. Lazzie had been through a lot with us and deserved to be treated well.

We pulled up to a street in one of the developments for rich alums who wanted to have second homes to convince themselves that they were still in college. "You live in Glory Days?" I asked.

"I live where?" he asked, somehow managing to seem offended.

"It's what Spencer calls this area because it's full of varsity sports alumni trying to relive their glory days. She says the water pressure is so good because there are so many tears when we lose a football game."

"Have you and Spencer tried not renaming everything?" He pulled into an underground garage and parked the car. "And my parents bought the house as an investment. I just live here. You need help carrying that in?" Lucas asked, nodding towards my backpack. "Seems like it might be heavy enough to take out a small army."

"Ha," I replied, rolling my eyes at him. "I carry it to class every day without a problem, so I think I should be able to get it into your apartment without a problem either."

"I just want to make sure that you don't throw out your back or something. You almost gave yourself a concussion on a sidewalk, so I should be concerned. And you could be hiding a Mack truck in there."

How original, a joke about my last name. "Shut up, Lucas *Wolf*." I hiked my backpack up onto my bag and started to follow him up towards the door.

"Has anyone ever told you – "

"If you make a joke about mack trucks right now, or Mac computers, or anything else, I'm going to lose it to you," I warned.

He shrugged and pushed open the door in front of it, holding it open for me. "You're missing out, mac and cheese"

I resisted the urge to stick my tongue out at him. Jokes about my last name had to be one of the least original things I've ever heard. It didn't help that my parents literally owned a chain of car dealerships.

"Sit down," he said, guiding me towards the couch.

"I am fully capable of – "

"Arielle, there is blood running down your legs and staining your shoes. Sit the hell down," he barked back.

I swallowed and let him support me until we got to the couch. His hand rested on my back, just lightly enough to guide me.

"Let me go take my tights off," I said, swallowing again.

He stared at me for a second, his pupils widening. "I'll go get the band-aids from the bathroom, and you can get changed while I'm gone," he said, his eyes not leaving me. "I don't think you should walk around in case you reopen the scab or something."

I glared at him, but he ignored me and walked out of the room. I reached down and took my shoes off, then started the process of pulling my tights off.

God, this was painful. They had stuck to my legs when I'd scraped them. I closed my eyes against the pain as I ripped them off. This was awful.

I bundled up the tights into a ball and stuffed them into my backpack. I wasn't throwing them away in Lucas's house, but they were wrecked. I was going to have to find a new favorite pair of tights now.

"Can I come back?" Lucas called from the next room.

"Yeah," I called back, sitting down on the couch and examining my legs. I had banged them up a lot worse than I had expected.

"Stretch your legs over my lap," he said, scooting towards me.

I wanted to protest but just nodded and did what he asked. He reached down and spread ointment on my legs. I closed my eyes, ignoring the sparks that were running up and down my legs now. This was clearly just because I hadn't been together with anyone since He Who Shall Not Be Named.

I wasn't going to think about that. I had learned how to take care of myself. That was more important.

"Hold still," Lucas said. I opened my eyes to see him opening up the band-aids, pressing them gently onto my legs. "You really hurt yourself, Arielle."

I had, but I was totally capable of taking care of myself afterwards, I wanted to say. "If you had to see Mason naked, you'd have done the same."

"Of course I've seen Mason naked," he said, starting to spread the ointment on my other leg. "The gym has communal showers."

"Don't tell me any more," I said, shaking my head. "I really don't want to know about naked Mason. Let me keep my mental image of him as a nerdy dentist wannabe."

He laughed, reaching for my hand and then cradling it in his. "I'm going to put ointment on these, too. I don't want you to get an infection from your fall."

I nodded. There was a not small, traitorous part of my brain that was enjoying this too much. But I had relied on a guy in the past, and that hadn't ended well.

He finished putting on the band-aids, and I swung my legs, landing back on the floor. I stood up. "Thanks," I said, my face flushing. I had to say thank you, but part of me didn't even want to say that and admit it.

"Do you want something to drink? We can study here until it's time to go to pizza night. Assuming that Raleigh and Mason aren't too busy for pizza night," he said, starting to reach a hand towards me and then stopping.

"That sounds great," I said, starting to walk into the kitchen. My legs ached with every step, as though I needed another reminder of my fall. Great going, Arielle.

I stopped as I walked into the kitchen. "Lucas." I pointed towards the entire counter that was just filled with the biggest, fanciest espresso maker than I had ever seen. "You know that I love coffee. You know that I trained as a barista last year. And you didn't bother to tell me that you have the greatest set up of all time?"

"You were training to be a barista last year?" he asked, following me into the kitchen.

"Yeah," I said, walking over and starting to touch all of the dials. "I needed a job and figured that being a barista couldn't be that hard. I was wrong." Apparently there was a subtle difference between a latte and a reverse cappuccino, whatever the hell that was. "At least it was fun. I'm a terrible artist, but I discovered that I'm actually really good with latte art."

"Now that you've said that, you're going to need to prove that," he said. He walked over towards me in a few giant steps.

"You have skim milk?" I asked, getting away from him as fast as I could and heading over towards the fridge. "Real skim milk. Not the imitation stuff. You can't make good latte art with oat milk."

"No one can, or you can't?" he asked. Out of the corner of my eye, I could see him leaning back against the countertops, watching me as I dug through the fridge to find the milk. Of course Lucas had fresh vegetables and classy beer in his fridge. He'd have to be evicted from Glory Days if his fridge had week old takeout in it.

I shut the fridge and brought over the skim milk. "Why haven't you had us over here? This is so much more comfortable than trying to squeeze in at Raleigh's."

He shook his head. "It's my parents' house. It feels weird having people over."

"Still." I started to search through the cabinets, looking for a cup to froth milk in. "Where do you keep the espresso stuff?"

"Here you go," he said, wrapping his arm around my front to pass me a container of ground coffee.

"Thanks," I said, starting up the machine. "Can you bring me mugs? I want to practice a few things."

"As long as I get a fancy coffee out of it," he said, turning back towards the counter. I took a deep breath and focused back on the coffee machine. I could handle this.

After I made us both lattes, including a tiny foam cat on the side of the cup, I sat down at the kitchen counter. I took a sip of my latte and forced myself to stare at my laptop, ignoring Lucas sitting across from me. Regency romance. I could do this.

Most students worked jobs at bars or serving tables or something to help cover the bills. I wrote. I wrote the kind of Regency romance novels that had half-naked men and women in giant frilly dresses on the covers. I wrote things with titles like *The Duke Who Dumped Me*, despite the fact that using dumping in that way wasn't exactly historically accurate.

It had started in high school, when I'd written a bunch of fanfiction about a TV show that I had loved. It was historical fiction, and it had insisted on having a happy ending, despite the fact that nothing was supposed to be lining up for that. It just wasn't believable that the entire cast would have managed to escape the sinking of the Titanic.

I had complained about it so much that my mom had told me, in one of her usual, emotionally sensitive pep talks, "Stop complaining if you can't do any better."

So I'd done better. Maybe a professional editor wouldn't have thought so, but I thought it was a real improvement. At the very least, I'd made all the misogynistic characters die of dysentery in chapter eighteen. I'd posted it online, and then, I'd joined a whole community of people who hated what had happened to the show.

It was so much fun that pretty soon, I was taking all of the secondary characters and giving them their own stories. And the comments kept me going. A few of them were mean, but most of the people really seemed like they were enjoying what I was writing.

It was kind of amazing, to be honest.

And then, everything had really changed when Athena Brigette had found me. She'd had more of a following than she could keep up with, and she wanted to have more time to branch out into other things. So she'd hired a small army of ghostwriters to help.

The pay was good in comparison to being a barista, and most of the time, too, it was fun to write. The books were always slightly over the top, but you know what you were getting when you picked up a book with a half naked duke on the cover.

Not, of course, that I had told anyone about this particular job. Not even Raleigh and Spencer.

Most people were embarrassed to admit that they picked up and enjoyed Athena's books. Which was ridiculous, because romance was actually an important genre. There was a reason they were the best selling books out there.

It wasn't that people read them because they were fluffy all of the time. Romance novels could help you see a better world, a better relationship. They could give people the confidence to know what they wanted from their relationships, and how to go get it.

I'd tried to explain this once to Nate, better known as He Who Shall Not Be Named. He'd stared at me for a second and then snorted. "You're telling me you think the people who write the stupid books you buy at airports are changing the world."

So now I just stuck with telling people I was an English and communications major. Communications was my major because my parents had insisted on it, because didn't I know the statistics about English majors getting jobs, and shouldn't I be more focused on my future?

Well. It was a good thing that I had a backup. Sure, it'd be fun to write my own stuff some day, but I wasn't anywhere near good enough to do that and actually live off it.

I focused back on the document for a little bit longer. I had gotten another page out before my phone vibrated with a group text from Raleigh. *Sorry everyone, but I got caught up with some stuff. Pizza night next week?*

Lucas and I both snorted at the same time. "That was the worst apology text I've ever gotten," I said, looking down at it. "But if there's no pizza night, I should head back to Spencer."

"Yeah," Lucas said, shaking his head. "Let me drive you home, at least."

I am independent and I don't need you to do that, part of me said, but then the other part won out. The part that maybe liked him. "Thanks."

Chapter 3

"Are you going over to Raleigh's?" Spencer asked, looking up from where she'd completely taken over the living room floor with various robot parts.

It had been three days since the incident, and I hadn't been able to bring myself to drop by Raleigh's apartment. I never wanted to see Mason naked or think about Mason naked or even have those two words anywhere near each other in my brain. I could write sex scenes, but in real life? No thanks.

"I guess that I have to look her and Mason in the face again at some point." At some point, I would get this image out of my brain and not immediately think of it every time I saw her. Maybe at her wedding. Or the birth of her first child. That seemed like the right timeline.

Spencer shrugged. "Or not. You had one embarrassing encounter in your entire friendship, so you should never speak to each other again in your life. That's my advice."

"Spence, no offense, but your advice is sometimes really not helpful." I dug through my bag, looking for my phone charger.

"I'm just saying that you should think about how embarrassing this actually is," she replied, scrunching her legs up. "You've seen plenty of penises before. You took art history freshman year."

"It doesn't count if it's for class!" She raised an eyebrow at me, and I threw one of the throw pillows towards her. "I should have texted her and made sure. She probably hates me now."

"Snap out of it. At least you'll get apology baked goods out of this," Spencer said, looking back down at her various parts. "Can you pass me a screwdriver?"

I passed her one, and she immediately started screwing together two of the tiny parts on the floor. "You're sure that you don't want to join?" I asked, pulling on the extremely ugly but extremely warm jacket I'd found at the campus thrift shop last year. It looked like the Michelin man had dyed himself pale pink, but you could survive Antarctica in it.

"I would, but I actually have to go lead a study group in half an hour." Spencer had the best teaching assistant gig in the whole school. One of her physics professors had pulled her aside sophomore year and told her that she was too smart to be in the back of the room, and she should be up front teaching. Spencer had dithered about taking it until she heard the salary.

"Have fun teaching. Don't get any declarations of love this time," I said, standing up and putting on my backpack.

"That was a one time thing," she called back at me as I pushed open the door and headed out of the apartment. "And I would appreciate it if you didn't bring it up."

Technically it had been a three time thing, but I wasn't going to turn around and correct her now. Spencer was a badass woman in STEM, which unfortunately meant that her male students either tried to mansplain her own topics to her or developed mad crushes on her.

It had been a real pain when I'd been dating Nate. Because the universe loved irony, Nate was always convinced that I was cheating on him. I'd had to go the extra length to show him I wasn't. I told him lots of stories about how pathetic all the guys who wanted Spencer were, even though at the end of the day, it was me who was the pathetic one.

I started the walk down the street towards Raleigh's apartment. It was a cold and gray day, and I pulled my jacket tighter around myself. I headed into Raleigh's building and up the stairs. I knocked on her door as loudly as I could. If Mason was naked, this was going to give him enough time to put on clothes.

Raleigh opened the door. "I'm so sorry," she said, holding out a sheet cake with the words *Sorry You Saw My Boyfriend Naked* written on them in bright pink script.

"You got me a cake?" I stared down at it for a second. This was a first. "Because I had to see Mason naked?"

"I'm so sorry. I know that I should have had my phone on loud, or locked the door, or something. And I am so embarrassed."

"There's no way that you're more embarrassed than I am." That probably didn't make her feel better, now that I thought about it. God, if someone had caught me with Nate, I would have locked myself in my room for weeks.

"Well, that's debatable. Anyway, I was embarrassed enough that I decided that I should bake you a cake or something to make up for it, so – here's the cake."

I stared down at the sheet cake. There were tiny flowers all around the sides of it and a marzipan topper. She'd really gone all out. "Raleigh, you're the best."

"If it makes you feel better, Mason was no happier about the whole situation. He came back into the room and was barely able to talk to me because he was so embarrassed about it. Really ruined the moment."

"Thanks. That was way more than I wanted to

know." I didn't need that mental image on top of everything else. "Should I get plates for this cake?"

Lilyanna came sniffing over, and Raleigh lifted the cake above her head to keep it away from the dog. "Lilyanna! How did you manage to get out of your room?"

"I told you, I think she's big enough to get over the baby gate." Lilyanna had developed a taste for fondant icing and loved to steal things off the counter when Raleigh was stress baking. You had to respect a dog who knew what she wanted.

"I'm not buying a bigger baby gate," Raleigh replied. She stuck the cake on the far corner of the counter Lilyanna couldn't reach, then reached down and scratched Lilyanna on the head. "I refuse to. Lilyanna needs to get smaller. Or dumber. Or something."

"Come on. You don't actually want a different dog," I said. I sat down at the table, and Lilyanna immediately laid her head in my lap. "You're the best. Who's the best dog? You're the best dog."

"And to think, you said that you didn't like dogs when I first got her," Raleigh said.

"We've been through some shit together," I said, scratching Lilyanna's head again. There had been a lot of nights after things fell apart with Nate when I'd been over at Raleigh's apartment, crying into Lilyanna's fur and thinking of what might have been.

It was not an exaggeration that this dog had

gotten me through. Unlike humans, dogs didn't tell you that the guy was an asshole and to stop crying. They just cuddled with you until you felt better.

"You just don't want to admit that you were wrong about dogs this whole time," Raleigh replied. She brought over two plates and forks and cut open the cake, which had layers of raspberry, whipped cream, and chocolate on the inside.

"What did I ever do to deserve you as my friend?" I asked, poking at the cake with my fork. "This cake is amazing."

"I've been practicing." Raleigh was a biomedical engineering major, which was notoriously one of the toughest majors on campus. The great thing for me was that she had decided that the best way to cope with the stress was to bake. She sighed. "I talked to Miriam yesterday."

And I'd been so stuck in my own head about the Mason incident that I'd missed it. Going for the shit friend award on top of everything. "Is everything okay?"

She nodded. "Things are tough, but they're getting better, you know?"

Raleigh's best friend in high school had been in a car accident, and then had been in a situation where everything had spiraled downhill. She'd ended up with a painkiller prescription that became addictive. Raleigh had been by her side for the entire time, and it still really hurt for her.

"And you're sure that you're okay?"

Raleigh ran a hand through her hair. "I think she might be able to kick it this time. The sickness, I mean. It's been so many years that I almost don't want to hope, you know? I don't know if I can let myself hope too much and then get worried again."

I nodded. "I'm here if you ever want to talk, Ray."

She looked down at her cake and poked it a few more times with her fork. "So now that we've talked about the thing that's hard for me to talk about, are we going to talk about your thing?"

"No thanks, I'm good." I reached over and took another piece of cake for myself, because it would be a crime to not eat this cake.

She stared at me, her mouth full of cake. "Arielle."

"Raleigh."

"Arielle."

"You can keep saying my name," I replied, stabbing the cake with a lot more force than was necessary to cut off a new piece. "We really can change the topic to something that's more pleasant to talk about."

"We can, but you know that you have to talk about N – "

"He who must not be named," I interrupted. There was a stupid part of me that still felt queasy and angry thinking about him. Best way to deal with that was to not say his name.

She fixed me with a glare. "I love Harry Potter, too, but he is not Voldemort. His name is Nate."

Ouch. My stomach clenched, and I closed my eyes for a second. Raleigh cleared her throat. "I know that you think you've gotten closure on the whole thing," she said, her voice soft.

"The only remaining closure I want is for him to reimburse me for the medical bills." I hadn't wanted to use my parents' insurance for an STD test, not when I wasn't sure if they were going to get the bill and be able to see what was going on. So I'd paid out of pocket at the student health center, and it had drained my savings. American healthcare was the best in the world, sure.

Raleigh sighed, sliding another piece of cake onto my plate. "I know, but it's been a year, and you still can't talk about him. And you haven't been out with anyone else, and it feels like you're avoiding that."

I took a deep breath. "I don't need to go out with people to move on from Nate. I have moved on. I learned my lesson."

If Raleigh wasn't going to let me call him He Who Shall Not Be Named, I'd go for the next best option. Having *Voldemort* as my boyfriend was the reason that my grades had plummeted, that I didn't have college friends outside of Spencer and Raleigh.

Six years. Six goddamn years. I had thought that it was going to be my happily ever after, that we were going to turn into the couple who everyone came to our wedding and wished that they were us. We had a plan. Things were going to work out.

And then Voldemort had destroyed it all. Exploded it all. Shattered it all. I didn't have enough synonyms to describe it properly.

I took another deep breath. "I know that I missed so many things with you guys. I missed Spencer's foam party, where she had the robot go crazy, and I missed the night you climbed the roof with Mason, and I missed taking that Jane Austen Revolutionary class because it was Friday afternoons."

I'd had to spend my weekends with Voldemort when we were dating, and he wasn't interested in coming to visit me in the cold when he told me I could just fly down to the University of Southern California. He wasn't interested in board game nights and baking with Raleigh. So of course, I'd gone along with it.

"You did miss those things, but that's not because of anything you did wrong," Raleigh said, her voice still soft and reasonable. Because she was a reasonable person, which of course made her even more annoying to argue with.

"But I don't want to miss those things again!" New Ari was independent and didn't have a man in her life. I wasn't going to depend on someone who let me down. "I don't need someone to do things for me. I have absolutely zero desire to put myself out there. I want to hang out with you and finish college strong. My grades are finally turning around."

"You can be yourself, date again, and still be strong and independent. What happened with Nate is something that you learned from and isn't going to happen again," she said, taking a bite of her cake.

Sure. But I felt like I'd just found Arielle again, and I wasn't ready to leave that. I finally knew who I was. I finally liked myself. Arielle, not just Nate's girlfriend.

I reached for the cake and took another piece. "I know." Raleigh looked over at me, and I swallowed. I had to give her something and convince her that things were okay with me. "But I promise. I'm taking full advantage of college. And I can't imagine any friends better than you guys."

Chapter 4

Usually I wouldn't consider myself too much of a coward. I mean, I published my writing on the internet. And there were a lot of trolls on the internet. But for some reason, the door to Raleigh's apartment was scaring me right now.

"Are you going to open the door or not?" Spencer asked. She was leaning against the wall behind me, snickering to herself.

"I have opened the door in the past." She was now not being the most supportive that she could be in the moment. It was just that the last time I came over, it was to hang out with Raleigh, not everyone. Everyone included Mason.

"Are you worried that Mason is going to make comments about the fact that you ran into him while he was naked? Or are you worried because now you will never be able to imagine him not naked again?"

she asked, one corner of her mouth turning up in a smirk. "Because I honestly don't know which one you should be more worried about."

"I just want to make sure that we're not interrupting anything." Oh god, and the mental image was coming back. I did not appreciate my brain sometimes.

"We are creepily standing in the hallway because you are afraid to ring the doorbell," she replied. "Come on. You are making the situation worse for yourself right now."

She had a point. I swallowed and rang the doorbell.

Mason opened the door. He looked at me, his face turning bright red. "Uh, hi, Arielle," he said, staring down at the floor.

"Arielle was just hoping that she'd see you naked again," Spencer said, sticking out her tongue at me as she walked in.

She was such a little jerk sometimes. "Absolutely not. Don't worry, Mason, I have no desire to ever have to see you naked again. It was a terrible experience."

"Ouch. Do you need some aloe for that burn, Mason?" Spencer asked. Lilyanna started to run circles around the two of us, and Spencer reached down and started petting her. "Hi, baby."

"Sometimes I think that you're more excited to come over and see my dog than me," Raleigh said, turning away from the counter, where she was preparing a tray of cupcakes. "I would be insulted if I didn't also think that she was the cutest thing in the world."

"She's the best," Spencer replied, kneeling down and starting to pet Lilyanna. "She's basically just a giant pool of fluff. How can you not fall in love with the giant pool of fluff?"

Mason scratched Lilyanna's head as he walked by us. I walked over to the counter and started to poke the cupcakes. "These look great."

"I still haven't gotten the flavors quite right," she said, shaking her head. "I was going for rose petals, but I think that I made it way too subtle in the cake. It's totally overpowered by the frosting."

"Do you have a problem set for physics that you're putting off right now?" Spencer asked, looking up from where she was still crouching on the floor and playing with Lilyanna.

"Yes, why?" Raleigh asked, licking frosting off one of her fingers.

"Cupcakes normally mean physics, and things with chocolate usually mean math," Spencer replied. "You're becoming predictable."

Raleigh stopped, staring at Spencer for a few seconds. Then she nodded. "You're actually right. I never noticed."

My friends were way too smart for me. I decided that the best answer for this was having a cupcake.

"Oh, I get the first one," Spencer said, reaching over towards my cupcake.

"Leave Arielle's cupcake alone, Spence. There are plenty for all of you," Raleigh said, swatting at both of us with her dishtowel.

"Arielle's here?" Oh shit. I knew that voice. I turned to see Lucas walking out of the side bedroom, wearing a t-shirt that looked perfectly worn in.

The scene that I had tried to write yesterday started to run through my head. *Lord Bennington stepped towards me, his hands huge and surprisingly soft. The hands of a man who could afford the finer things in life. In my mind, I started to think of those hands touching me, on my —*

Nope. Nope, nope, nope.

"Are we all stealing Ari's cupcakes? Is this our new game?" he asked, taking a step towards me. My traitorous heart did a little bit of a flutter.

"Don't even think about it. I made enough for everyone." Raleigh swatted at Lucas with her dishtowel, and he grinned back at her.

"You must have really been trying to get away from having to actually do your homework," Spencer said, reaching over and swiping a fingerful of frosting from my cupcake.

"What the hell?" I asked, looking down at my formerly beautifully frosted cupcake. This was the worst game. "Spence!"

"Is your knee doing better?" Lucas asked, leaning on the counter and looking directly at me.

"Arielle's knee?" Raleigh asked, immediately switching into overprotective friend mode.

"It's really nothing. I just tripped yesterday, and Lucas gave me a band-aid. It's all better now," I said, trying to end this topic.

"Lucas gave you a band-aid," Raleigh repeated, looking over at Spencer. Spencer smirked.

Changing the topic. I crouched down on the floor next to Lilyanna and ruffled the fur behind her head. She tilted her head up and licked my nose. "Ew." I leaned back and away from her. "I don't love you that much."

"Lil, here," Lucas said, holding his hand down and snapping his fingers. She immediately left me and trotted over to Lucas, sitting down next to him so that he could stroke her head.

"How did you do that?" I asked, looking up at him. "She never listens to me."

"She listens to the people who take her out for lots of miles," he replied, raising an eyebrow at me. "You should try it. It's the fastest way to her heart."

"I'll stick with my normal length jogs around the block." Lilyanna had developed a thing about the word walk, and she might get too excited and knock you over if she heard it. I'd gotten really good at picking synonyms.

"Need a hand getting up?" he asked, extending his hand towards me as I crossed my legs to stand up.

I closed my eyes for a second, trying to resist the

urge to reach up and pull his face down towards mine. It had been so much easier when I'd been dating Voldemort. Because then I had ignored any feelings that might have been developing for Lucas. I wasn't going to even think about cheating on my significant other. I wasn't that kind of person.

Even if Voldemort was.

"How is your communications class going?" Raleigh asked, looking over at me. I leaned against the counter.

"It's fine." It was with a professor who everyone knew was mean, the kind of person who had gone into teaching so that he could tell people they were wrong all day long.

"You said last year that you were thinking about dropping the major rather than having to take it," Raleigh said, pausing at the kitchen sink.

"You'd drop the major rather than take this class?" Lucas asked, taking a step towards me.

"The professor is a jerk. But I'm only one class away from finishing the major," I said. I only had to get through senior seminar, and then I would never have to write another press release in my life. Or another marketing tweet.

"But you're an English major too," Raleigh said, her eyes meeting mine.

"I just feel like it's something I should do because English isn't practical." My parents had reminded me of that enough times. My dad had even done the neat trick of refusing to pay for any credit hours that he didn't think would lead to a career later.

Spencer snorted. "And you think that physics is always practical? Do what you love, Arielle. We have plenty of time to figure out practicalities later. And you deserve to be happy with what you have to do all day every day."

I nodded, the words not coming. My friends were almost too supportive sometimes. I could have told Spencer that my desire was to become a professional trapeze artist despite my total lack of hand-eye coordination, and she would have signed up for courses right alongside me.

Mason pushed open the door, and the entire apartment started to smell like pizza. "God, this smells amazing," Spencer said, walking over to the counter and opening the first box.

"I think it's a rule with pizza. Pizza will always smell amazing, no matter if it's the best or the worst pizza in the world. You can't have bad pizza," I replied.

"That is false. I have had bad pizza before in my life, and it was awful. And it is worse than you can imagine, because you get your hopes up for good pizza," Spencer replied, taking a piece. Lucas passed her a stack of paper towels. "Bad pizza. That's a great low-karma punishment. Have shitty pizza. It doesn't create long term emotional distress, but it gets the point across."

"Have I mentioned that you're weird?" Mason asked, reaching for his own piece of pizza.

"Your life goal is to be a dentist. You can't talk," Spencer replied, tossing a napkin at him.

Over the pizza, my eyes caught Lucas's. And my traitorous stomach flipped a little bit.

Chapter 5

"It's going to be a good night," Spencer sang, completely off tune, as we started to pull on our clothes for going out that night.

"Remind me why we're going to a house party again? I have plenty of school work that needs to be done," I said, checking my dress in the mirror. I was making a major concession to the weather and wearing tights under my dress, despite the fact that I hated tights. My mom had made me wear pantyhose under my dresses for all of our family events, and even thinking about it made my skin crawl.

"Because we're in college, and I'm pretty sure that this is one of the things that you're supposed to do in college," she replied, leaning forward in the mirror and putting on lip gloss.

"We've literally never done anything because it's supposed to be what you do in college." I bent down and sorted through our joint closet, looking for shoes that were at all appropriate to wear to this kind of party. "Why are we starting now?"

"Do you want me to tell you it's because I want to hook up with one of the guys at the party? Because I will tell you that I want to do that if that's going to get you to shut up and go out with me." She glanced over at me, where I was pulling heeled boots out of the closet. "Those are mine."

"Damn it." Spencer and I were a foot size different, just enough that I could squish into her shoes in an emergency, but my feet would hurt the entire day afterwards. I was always tempted to wear her shoes. And then I would do it and regret it, and still, I would never learn.

"The guy throwing the party is in my exoplanets elective, and he's super cute," she said, holding her hair up and then letting it fall down again.

"So we're going to a party with a bunch of math nerds? What are we going to do, play board games and write dirty words on our calculators?" To be honest, that sounded kind of nice.

"Don't be silly. It's a party. It's going to be a house with a ton of people and they're going to have loud music," she replied. "It's like you forget all your friends are STEM majors."

"How did you know that eating pizza was going to be my ideal night out tonight?" I asked.

It was my ideal night out most nights, but especially today. I'd been working on the book all day, after getting a gentle reminder from the publisher that I was going to have to send in chapters soon. The words just weren't coming out right. The plot was supposed to be that Lady Beverly was resisting Lord Bennington because she didn't want to be trapped in a relationship – especially in the Regency period, where there were so many more rules about what that entailed. But I hadn't been able to get it quite right. She either sounded like she was being silly, or he was being too much of a jerk, or something. But this book was paying for my tuition this semester, so I needed to get on with the writing.

Spencer turned to face me, leaning against the dresser that we used as a makeup counter. "It's your senior year of college. Let's go have some fun. Otherwise, you're going to turn into one of those people who dies alone in her room after she has a heart attack and can't get up from the floor."

"That's a really detailed death that you just gave me." I dug through the closet a little more, looking for shoes that were actually in my size. I had a pronounced lack of going out clothing, because I'd spent most of my weekends in college with Nate. I'd bought clothes I knew Nate would like, and when we'd ended, I'd donated all of them.

"I need to be detailed, or you are going to do that thing again where you tell me you have so much work, and you stay on the couch watching things on your computer. Come on. Let's go out, drink bad beer, flirt with some overconfident and under-attractive guys, and then let's come back and gossip and eat mediocre pizza at two am." Spencer clapped her hands together and then stared at me.

I didn't have a choice in this plan, but at least there was now pizza in it. "You've decided this already, haven't you?" I asked.

She nodded. "I have. And having you come with me is a crucial part of this plan. Because you are my best friend, and I want to have fun with my best friend. We haven't gone out together enough, and we have to make up for lost time."

I was powerless against that argument. I shook my head and leaned down to zip up my boots. "Let's go then."

YOU COULD HEAR the music from the house before you could see it. And if that failed, you could just follow the trail of red Solo cups, lying on the grass like breadcrumbs. I turned towards Spencer. "And we're sure that – "

"Yes." Spencer turned towards me. "We are sure that this is the right party, and you have to do something social for once in this entire school year."

"And I guess that this is the way that we are going to do it," I said, taking a deep breath. "Let's go."

"That's my girl," Spencer said, grinning at me and nodding towards the door. "It's party time."

Inside, the party was already in full swing. There was a huge crowd of people shoved into the living room, and we could barely fit through the doorway. "This is a party?" I yelled at her.

"Shut up. It'll be better once we find something to drink," she replied, grabbing my hand and pulling me deeper into the house.

"Bryce!" Spencer bubbled as we reached the punch bowl. This was not a Spencer tone of voice. I tried to shoot her a look, but she avoided my eyes.

"Hello, girls," the guy said, spreading his arms wide. "Welcome to the party of the year."

I was not convinced that any party thrown by math majors could be the party of the year, but maybe I just hadn't gone to enough parties. "Let me get you something to drink," he said, reaching into the fridge. "The finest spiked seltzer in the land."

I'd barely drunk before, because when I went to parties with Nate, I was always the person who stayed sober to pick up the pizza or the extra beer. And Nate and his friends would play drinking games, which I was never invited to be part of. They were for the boys.

"Thanks," Spencer said. "Give us two, and we're going to go dance."

He nodded and passed us another two. Spencer

stuck them in the pockets of her jacket and raised an eyebrow at me. "Let's dance."

I followed her through the crowd towards the living room, where she passed me a seltzer. "Cheers," she said, cracking open the top of the first seltzer and clinking it against mine. "To getting out!"

"Getting out!" I called back, opening my seltzer. The music changed to a song that I actually knew, and I started nodding along.

Spencer reached over and spun me around on my heels, grinning at me. "See? This is fun!"

"Ari! Spence!" Someone grabbed me from behind, I turned around to see Luisa standing there, grinning at me. "You're here!"

"Luisa!" I wrapped her in a full hug, returning hers. Luisa was friends with Raleigh, and one of those people who I wished that I'd gotten to know better at the beginning of college. She was part of our friend group but not my close friend.

"Spencer told me that you were coming out." She leaned over and clinked her seltzer can against mine. "Cheers!"

"Cheers!" I clinked my can against hers, then took a sip.

"I'm so glad that you came out tonight," she said, leaning close to me and speaking directly in my ear. "I love Spencer, but she's rotten at the people watching game."

We'd invented this one back in sophomore year. I

pointed at a couple in the corner. "She's had a crush on that girl over there for years. She's using the guy she's with to make her jealous."

"Good one," Luisa said, nodding. "You can tell with the way she's leaning. She's not into the guy, and she keeps looking over at the girl over there."

"And I'm pretty sure that it's romantic and not friend jealousy, because the body language just screams I want to be in your bed," I said.

"Are you two playing your creeper game?" Spencer asked, throwing her arms around both of us. "Come on, let's dance!"

We danced through the next few songs, Spencer showing off her dance skills with the lawnmower and the velociraptor, patented Spencer dance moves. "You look like an idiot!" I shouted at her.

She responded by pawing at me with her dinosaur arms, and I pulled her into a hug. "Thank you," I said into her ear. "For getting me to come out."

I had missed this. I hadn't known how much I had missed this. She gave me another hug, squishing me against her. "That's what best friends are for!"

The music changed, and I joined Spencer in the worst dance moves of all time. Apparently Spencer's dance skills were a siren call for boys in Spencer's exoplanets class, because the guy from earlier came walking over, holding out another can of seltzer for her.

This felt like the right moment to step out. "I'm

going to go to the bathroom!" I shouted at Spencer and Luisa.

"Okay!" Luisa yelled back, blowing me a kiss. "I love you!"

I blew her a kiss back, then started to push through the crowd to find the bathroom. I found a hallway with a bunch of doors, which had to be the bedrooms and the bathroom in this house.

People really should have bathroom signs at these parties. I opened the door to the bathroom and stared down at the lock. It was the most complicated lock that I had ever seen, a bunch of different sliders and chains. I did all of them as well as I could and tested the door.

Yep, the door wasn't going to open while I was on the toilet. This was a good thing.

I reached the toilet and sighed with relief. I hadn't realized how much my feet were hurting. Honestly, it might not be a terrible idea to just hang out here for a couple of minutes, away from all of the noise of the party and where I could actually take my shoes off without worrying about stepping on something.

I was pretty sure that I had grabbed Spencer's shoes. Because they were very cute, and they hurt. A lot.

I washed my hands twice, because even if this was a math frat, it was still a frat house. I walked over to the door and started to undo the locks. It was even more complicated than I had thought coming in.

I started to pull the door open after the locks were open. It wouldn't budge.

I had opened all the locks, hadn't I? I looked down. Yep, I had.

The door was probably just stuck because of the humidity or something. It was all the shitty beer in the air. I grabbed the doorknob with both hands and pulled as hard as I could.

Unfortunately, the only thing that moved was the doorknob. It popped off the door, slipping out of my hands and rolling under the sink.

Shit. This wasn't good.

I banged on the door a few times. "Anyone able to let me out?"

Nothing. Just lots of bass from the party.

Okay, I wasn't going to panic. I had a friend who could pick any lock in existence. I grabbed my phone and hit Spencer's number.

It rang, and rang, then rang again. Oh no. She'd had her phone in the pocket of her jacket, because there were no pockets on her dress. And it was hot, so she'd probably taken off her jacket and put it somewhere.

Okay, Luisa. I hit her contact, and the same thing happened.

This was not good. In fact, this was straight bad.

I couldn't call Raleigh right now. I wasn't going to force her to interrupt date night with Mason to come get me out of the bathroom at a party.

But I didn't really have another choice. And she did owe me a favor after the Mason incident. Well then. I dialed her number, and she picked up immediately. "What's up?"

How did you tell your friend that you were basically a kindergartener and had gotten yourself stuck in a bathroom? "I could kind of use some help right now."

"What's wrong?" Raleigh's voice was immediately worried. "Are you okay? Where are you?"

"Is that Arielle?" came Lucas's voice over the phone. Damn it. Speakerphone should be banned.

Ugh, I had to say these words out loud. "I'm at a party with Spencer. But I sort of locked myself in the bathroom and I can't get out."

"You locked yourself in the bathroom?" Raleigh asked. She started laughing. "Oh my god, Ari."

"Where are you?" Lucas asked. "Are you okay?"

I was going to ignore him. "I didn't exactly lock myself into the bathroom, but I'm stronger than I thought. And I sort of tore the doorknob off the door."

"You managed to tear off a doorknob? I thought you pride yourself on being our unathletic friend," Raleigh replied.

I was going to take the small win here. "Yeah. Except when it comes to frat house bathrooms, apparently." Wait, that sounded deeply wrong. I was taking that back.

"Where is she?" Oh great, now Lucas was asking Raleigh questions instead of me.

"Where are you?" Raleigh repeated into the phone.

"I'm in the math frat house. In a bathroom on the first floor in one of the back wings to the right."

"Tell her I'm on my way," Lucas said in the background.

Oh god, no. I didn't need the help. I was Arielle, and I could take care of my own problems. "No, seriously – " I called.

Raleigh cut me off. "He's already walking out, Ari. You're sort of screwed here."

"I didn't want him coming and making this a big thing!" I had spent so long making sure that I could take care of myself. I didn't need to call a man to come fix things for me.

"Oh, I know. If you wanted Lucas to come riding in on a white horse, you could have just called him."

"Did you just use a literary reference? I'm so proud of you." I felt so much better now that I'd taken my shoes off and sat down again. Honestly, I could just stay in the bathroom all night and talk to Raleigh.

"It's a Taylor Swift song reference, actually," she replied.

Of course. "Well, partial credit."

I reached down and rubbed the bottom of my

feet. "Are you sure you're okay without me?" she asked again. Curse her worrying ways.

"Yes, totally." I wasn't turning this into a bigger deal than I already had. "Seriously, go enjoy your date night with Mason."

"If it makes you feel better, he and Lucas were playing video games, and I was studying. So maybe now we can actually talk," she replied. "If you need a silver lining for this situation."

"You can pay me back later with baked goods. Now go have a fun night." She laughed and hung up the phone, and I sat down on the bathtub edge and stretched my feet out. It felt so good to be off my feet. I was throwing these shoes back on Spencer's side of the closet as soon as I got home.

I closed my eyes for a second.

Then came the pounding on the window.

I leapt up, nearly smacking my head against the wall. "What?" I shouted. Who the hell was pounding on the window? What was this party?

"Arielle, open the window!"

Oh god. That was Lucas. I climbed over to the window and unlocked it, pushing it open. Lucas was standing on a lawn chair below.

"What are you doing here?" I yelled at him. His face was just under mine.

"Coming to get you out of here, obviously," he said. "Stand back." He reached up to the rim of the window, pulling himself up over and into the bathroom.

My throat was suddenly dry, staring at him standing there. He was wearing an old t-shirt and his normal khakis, slightly sweaty even in the cold.

"How the hell did you get yourself locked into the bathroom?" He ran his hand through his hair, his eyes on me. Then he looked down at my feet. "And why are you barefoot at a frat party?"

"They were Spencer's shoes, and I couldn't stand them any longer. Or stand in them any longer." I might have gotten myself stuck in a bathroom, but I was still great at puns. I pointed towards the door. "And you try opening the door without a doorknob."

He picked up the doorknob from the floor and walked back towards the door, staring at it. He was close enough that I could smell his soap and a little bit of sweat. It should not have been attractive. He tried to stick the doorknob back in. "Damn it. You're right."

"Why do you sound so surprised by that?" Just because I wasn't an engineer like all my friends didn't mean that I couldn't open doors. Most of the time, at least.

He ignored my comment and looked over my head back towards the wall behind us. "I think we're going to have to go out the window."

I hadn't even considered that. "That is a drop. You know that, right?" The house was slightly elevated, and slightly elevated made a pretty big difference when you were talking about having to jump out of a window.

"I'll go first, and I'll catch you," he said, taking a step towards me. Maybe it was the alcohol, but all of a sudden, I was way too aware of his presence, the way that he was stepping towards me and coming closer and closer.

I nodded, swallowing down the lump that had just started in my throat. "Okay. We can do that."

His hand skimmed over my arm, and I closed my eyes for a second. He held out his hand, and I walked over towards the window. He lowered the top of the toilet seat, and then looked back at me. "What you're going to have to do is push yourself up into the window, and then out and over. You should be able to step onto it pretty easily from here."

"Okay," I said, swallowing again. I stepped up onto the toilet and glanced out the window.

Lucas nodded, towards me and then pushed himself up and into the window ledge. He looked back at me before he swung his foot over and vanished out of the window.

If he could do it, I could do it too. I swallowed, then pushed myself up into the window ledge.

Oh god. It wasn't that far, but it was still slightly further than I was expecting. I hated heights.

"Come on," he said from below, staring up at me. "I'll catch up. I've got you, Arielle."

I closed my eyes for a second. Oh god. You couldn't die on a six foot drop, could you? Because I didn't want my obituary to read "died falling out of a frat house window."

I swallowed, then stared at the drop. The only way to do this was to do it.

I pushed myself off the ledge and down towards the ground. Lucas's arms wrapped around me as I started to touch the ground. His arms were stronger than I expected, and my whole body seemed to light up all of a sudden. Everything responded to him.

I stared up at him, my breathing heavy. "We did it!"

He stared down at me. I stared back up at him, our eyes meeting. "It's really hard not to kiss you when you look at me like that," he said, not moving away from me an inch.

And then I took matters into my own hands.

I pushed myself up onto my tiptoes, leaning my head back. Our lips met in the middle. His lips were soft and warm, and as soon as they touched mine, it was like an explosion in my chest. I couldn't stop myself, my hands started to go to the bottom of his shirt.

He groaned and pulled me closer. I wrapped my hand in the bottom of his shirt, closing my eyes and pressing closer and closer to him.

And then –

He tore away from me, stepping back. "Are you kidding?"

"What?" This was so ridiculous and unexpected. I thought I was over all the guys in the world, after Nate, but now I was here, and I wanted Lucas. I actually wanted to kiss him, to be with him. I could look at him and not think about Nate. This was amazing.

"You're drunk."

I stared back at him. "Only a little bit. I mean, I've only had a couple of drinks. I'm not drunk drunk."

"Fuck!" He leaned back and ran both hands through his hair, not looking at me.

I stared at him for a second. I didn't understand. I just wanted to kiss him because he was there, and I wanted him, and this was all so much. I hadn't done anything wrong. "I'm sorry," I whispered.

"Fuck, Ari!" He ran his hands through his hair again. "I like you, okay? I like you a lot. If you're going to kiss me, I want to know that you mean it and it's not some drunk thing!"

I stared at him. *I meant it,* I wanted to say. Because I had meant it. I hadn't expected it, but I had meant it.

He cleared his throat and looked away from me, running a hand through his hair again. "You are the only person I know who can manage to get themselves stuck in a bathroom at a party."

He was changing the topic before I could even

process what he'd said. But I couldn't go back now. "It's not an experience that I'm planning to repeat any time soon."

He shook his head and held out his hand towards me. "Let's go home. It's freezing out."

Chapter 6

Spencer stared down at a novel open on her lap. "Have I mentioned that I hate this class?"

"A few times," I replied, snuggling further into the living room couch. Sundays in school were always my least favorite. It used to be the day that I would do all my homework after spending the weekend with Nate, and now they were the days where I cranked out writing for my job.

I was supposed to send in the first half of *The Lord Who Loved Me* to my editor in a few days, and it just wasn't writing. I had typed words, but they weren't good words. I couldn't even get myself to care about the characters.

"I don't even know what compelled me to take this class," she said, staring down at her book again. "Someone should have warned me that science skills do not translate to anything else. You want me to read this and analyze it? No thank you. I think I need more coffee for this."

"You can try to start a couple cups," I offered. It was too bad that I hadn't figured out a way to steal Lucas's espresso maker, because Spencer and I were still using the little stovetop pot that we had found at a thrift shop sophomore year.

"I think this is a day that calls for getting the normal coffeemaker out from under the cabinets," she said.

"That kind of day?" I asked. The real coffeemaker had a habit of leaking onto the counter, and you had to daisy chain extension cords behind the TV to get it to work. It was only for days where we were very sad, hungover, or both.

She nodded and rolled her legs off the couch, standing up and heading over towards the cabinet. "You know, we really could just take out that coffee maker and keep it out somewhere. It would be a lot easier than the stovetop maker," I suggested.

Spencer shook her head, kneeling down to reach into the cabinet. "Are you kidding? Have you seen this kitchen? We definitely don't have the counter space."

"We could get another table or something?" I offered. We'd taken one Ikea trip when we'd first started living off campus, both of us piling into Lazzie and picking up everything that we thought we could need to make the house comfortable and a little bit fun. It had been a very fun trip, until we'd discovered that not all of the things that we had bought would fit in Lazzie

We'd bungeed corded the trunk shut to try to keep everything in. I'd had to climb into the backseat and hold onto the edge of the couch for the entire two and a half hour drive home, trying to make sure we didn't cause a flying couch collison.

In retrospect, it had not been the best idea that we had ever had.

"If you're thinking that we should make another Ikea trip, I'm going to tell you that it's a hard no on that one," she replied. "We could have killed someone on the highway with that couch."

"But we didn't. And that was the important thing." And now we had a very comfortable couch. Spencer's engineering skills had many practical applications.

"I am still not doing that again. That was not the way that I'm supposed to be using my engineering skills to help the greater good," she shot back. She pulled the coffee marker out of the cabinet and stared at it for a second. "Seriously, though, this thing is so much easier than the stovetop one."

"Because it is. You just put the coffee in and the water in, and then you press a button, and five minutes later, you have basically unlimited coffee. You don't have it stand over it and chant to hope that it doesn't overflow," I replied.

"It overflows once a month. Don't exaggerate.

And that was because you were tipsy when you decided that it was time to make coffee," she shot back.

Okay, that was a valid critique. "One time, Spence. That was one time."

She shrugged and started to drape extension cords across the floor. "And it's one time that I can still make fun of you for."

"This is why we're friends," I replied.

She knelt down behind the TV, looking around for the outlet. She plugged in the cord and then looked up, grinning at me. "And the same back to you."

We sat in stillness for a few seconds as the coffee maker started to run. "I love the sound of brewing coffee in the morning," Spencer said, staring at the machine in awe.

"So are you going to tell me about your night now that we have coffee?" I asked. She'd gotten home late last night, and I'd been half asleep when she'd walked in.

She pulled two mugs down from our properly low cabinet and filled them up. She walked back towards our side of the room, passing me one of the mugs. "Can I just say again that you have the world's worst luck to get locked in the bathroom?"

"You don't need to remind me." That was going to be a story that was passed around our friend group for a long time. That time that Arielle managed to drunkenly lock herself in a bathroom and had to jump out a window. A real classic. "You want to tell me about your night instead of having me relive that for the hundredth time?"

She grinned at me. "Honestly, I kind of think it'd be more fun for me to make you relive that again. Didn't Lucas have to come and help get you out the window?"

I swallowed. Great. We could relive the part where I required a Taylor Swift-level hero on a white horse to rescue me. "Yeah. He climbed in the window and then helped me get out when it was clear the lock was broken. It was actually kind of hot."

She banged her coffee cup down on the table at that, turning towards me and crossing her arms. "Are you going to explain that statement, Arielle Mack?"

I should have thought before opening my mouth there. "I'm cool just leaving that where it is."

She narrowed her eyes at me. "No, I think that you just admitted that Lucas is attractive to you, and that is a thing that we need to talk about a little more after the years of denial we've been dealing with here."

"It really isn't something that we need to talk about." Understatement of the year. My brain filled in the image of him pushing me away, turning away from me when I'd reached towards him. "It was just – it was weird at the end."

She completely pushed her book away and crossed her legs underneath her, looking at me and cradling her coffee with both hands. "I think this is the thing that we need to be talking about, Arielle."

I don't want to do this if you don't mean it. My stomach cramped together. "I think that he told me that he likes me."

"That is not a world changing event or anything," she said, taking a drink of her coffee. "We have known that for a long time. He's obviously into you. And he's been trying to be respectful of the fact that you don't seem to be into him in the same way."

"But I – " Oh god. I wasn't sure I was ready to admit this to Spencer.

"But?" she prompted, still not letting her eyes off my face. God, she could have been a CIA interrogator.

I swallowed. Now I had to admit to Spencer that I'd gotten rejected. I'd actually tried to make a move on someone, and they'd shut me down. "I might have kissed him last night."

She slammed her hand down on the table hard enough that coffee flew everywhere. "I knew it!"

"How did you know what?" I demanded.

"As soon as you told me that he had come to rescue you from the bathroom, I knew what was going to happen. It was like one of those cliché romance novels. He rode in on his white horse and rescued you."

I was literally trying to write that scene at the moment, complete with white horse, so I didn't appreciate her description of it as the most cliché thing ever. "It wasn't like that."

"So are you going to explain what it was like instead?" she asked. "Because you know, there are a lot of details that you seem to be leaving out of this story. And I will remind you that it is basically the roommate code of ethics that you always disclose the details of any story that involves potential romantic partners."

"Since when has that been part of the roommate code of ethics?" I asked, reaching for my coffee again.

"I just added it. So please share this one without getting your knickers in a twist."

"What show did you steal that expression from?"

"I watch British television, Arielle." She crossed her arms, staring at me even more intently. "Tell me what happened between you and Lucas last night. I will remind you that I plugged in the coffeemaker, despite all the cobwebs behind the TV, and therefore you owe me one."

That shouldn't count, but Spencer was not going to get caught up on technicalities this morning. I sucked in a breath. "I might have kissed Lucas last night. And that was sort of a mistake."

"Why on earth would that be a mistake?" she demanded.

Because I had seen his face last night when I'd tried to kiss him. "I think he's pretty pissed at me right now."

She stood up, moving onto the couch next to me and crossing her legs. "Do you want to explain the things you're saying, or just keep talking around them?"

"When I got stuck in the bathroom – and no thanks to you, please remember to keep your phone on loud and with you during parties, thanks – he helped me get out the window. But then I kissed him, and he was pissed." I could still remember that part perfectly. Him pushing me away and telling me he didn't want it.

"Again, I'm going to need some more explanation here." Spencer turned so that she could stare directly into my eyes.

"Because I was drunk!" I shook my head. "He thought that that meant that I was doing it just because I was drunk, and then told me he didn't want to kiss me if I wasn't into it."

"Were you into it?"

The butterflies started in my stomach again. It was like I was fourteen or something, getting excited about the prospect of just kissing someone. "Yes?"

Spencer leaned towards me, her voice softer. "And so your problem with this is?"

"I just – " I shook my head. "I don't think I'm ready to date anyone. I want to take care of myself and put myself first and know who I am. I want to be Arielle Mack, not somebody's girlfriend."

"Liking him doesn't mean you have to give up

your identity." She reached for her coffee cup, taking a sip.

"You know what happened before." I was still trying to make up for all the time that I had lost.

"Not every guy is Nate. He was a piece of shit, and you didn't know better. You're stronger and know more now than you did then, Ari. You can have Lucas and be the best version of Ari, too."

"I lost college because I was dating someone. And I could have lost so much more." I still heard the voice. *You don't think you're going to make money with those stupid books, are you? Try getting a better hobby next time.*

"Lucas isn't Nate. He doesn't expect you to go home and help him do his laundry." Spencer had never forgiven Nate for that specific incident. "You gave that piece of shit a lot of love and care that you never got back. But that's not everyone. That's him."

I swallowed. I couldn't even think about Nate without my pulse speeding up and my palms getting sweaty, but not in a good way. "It doesn't matter. Lucas is pissed at me anyway."

"You get it, though." She took another sip of her coffee, leaning back and looking at me.

"What do you mean, you get it?" Spence seemed to be forgetting that she was sworn to be on my side in this. Roommate code of ethics and what not.

"Drunk people cannot consent. You have told him that you are not interested in him. Then you kiss him. And then, he is very confused. So he wants to make sure that he's dealing with the sober version of you that knows what it wants and can consent to things. It's straightforward enough," she replied.

Oh. If I thought talking to Spencer was going to make me feel better, I was wrong. I had never thought about it that way. He liked me enough that he didn't want to kiss me. He didn't want me to think that it was a drunken hookup for him. It mattered.

I couldn't process all of this right now. "We're changing the topic. How was last night for you?"

Spence sighed and ran her hand through her hair. Oh dear. This wasn't going to be good. "You know the guy Bryce who we ran into before you had your bathroom adventure?"

I wasn't sure that I liked the fact that we were referring to it now as my bathroom adventure, but I didn't think that I was going to win that argument. "Yeah. What happened to him?"

She shook her head. "I don't think that anything is going to happen there. It's just — it's frustrating. Because I like him, and I think that he likes someone else."

"Oh, Spence, I'm sorry." That sucked. It was the feeling of giving and giving, asking for scraps in return, and not even getting a crumb. I knew that feeling from Nate quite well.

She shrugged, looking down towards her coffee. "He told me last night after we hooked up that 'he didn't want it to be a big serious thing', you know?

And that to me was like, okay. But then I was thinking about it, and I don't think I'm okay with that. I want to have a relationship if I'm going to hook up with him. Because I actually like him."

I nodded, wrapping my hands around my coffee cup. "I know."

I don't want this if you don't mean it.

"I'll refill your coffee," I said, standing up and grabbing both cups. I walked over the machine.

"Thanks," Spencer said as I walked back, holding out her cup. "What are you working on?"

I sat down on the couch and looked down at my computer. *The Lord Who Loved Me (working title).docx* was still on the front screen. "An essay for Professor Li."

"Sounds boring as hell." She pulled her book back towards her, and I looked back down at my computer.

I pushed my long skirts out of the way. Wait, could you push a hoop skirt back? I should check. Athena Brigette fans would make you sure you knew if you messed up any historical details. I'd once gotten a barrage of emails because I described the wrong shade of yellow.

"Wait, you're writing an essay for what class?"

I glanced up at Spence, barely looking away from my computer screen. I'd pulled up the Wikipedia article on women's fashion in the Regency period and was starting to skim through it. "Professor Li." I was almost sure I had said Professor Li before.

"I thought you told me last week that you didn't

have a paper for that class, because you were only going to have a final presentation," she said.

Shit. That was right. "Um – "

But before I could say anything else, she'd jumped up and snatched my laptop out of my hands. "Give that back!" I called, leaping to my feet.

"Nope," she said, holding my laptop over her head and taking a step back. "Tell me what you're actually doing."

"Why are you so suspicious all of a sudden?" I could totally lie to her. I had never managed it before, but I could do it now. "Maybe I was just procrastinating."

She stared at me, narrowing her eyes. "If you were procrastinating, you would have told me what it was. And if it was porn, you would be in your room, and you definitely wouldn't be sitting here looking frustrated. So it's either Lucas's Instagram – "

"I am not looking at Lucas's Instagram!"

"So are you going to tell me, or I am going to have to read for myself?"

Remember what you said about cliche romance novels earlier? "You are not seriously trying to blackmail me right now. That's my laptop. It's private."

"And you're lying to me." She kept the laptop hoisted into the air. "I'm going to actually get worried that it's something bad if you keep not telling me."

That was not how this was supposed to work. There was a human right to privacy. But there were also roommate rules, and I could either tell her now or hear about this forever. Oh god. I closed my eyes and took a deep breath. "Please don't make fun of me for this."

"It's furry porn, isn't it? Please don't tell me that you've been watching furry porn and secretly getting off this whole time."

Yep, Spencer would come up with a story that was even more embarrassing than the truth. "No kink shaming."

"No changing the topic," Spencer replied, shutting my laptop and tucking it under her arm.

Argh. She knew me too well. "Fine." I took another deep breath and closed my eyes again. Might as well get this conversation over with. "So you know that some people write fan fiction?"

"Seriously, this is all about some fanfiction?" she said, placing my computer gently back on the couch. "You are this embarrassed about fanfiction? Is it terribly written slash fiction?"

"How do you even know that term?" I didn't think that anyone outside of the fanfiction community knew about that particular brand of erotica.

"I contain multitudes," she replied, sitting back down on the couch next to my laptop. "So all of that was because of fanfiction?"

I swallowed. "Well, that's where it started."

"And then it moved onto furry porn," she droned

in her best David Attenborough impression. She glanced up at my face, then snorted. "Sorry, I'll stop."

"There is no furry porn involved with any of this!" I wasn't sure what it meant that my roommate jumped to that conclusion. "Some of my fanfiction actually got noticed, and I got an offer to ghostwrite professionally. So I've been writing romance novels, like the kind that only come out in paperback that you buy at the airport, for the past couple years. I get paid for it, and it's how I'm paying for the tuition my parents don't cover."

"Are you serious?" Spencer stared at me. "Really?"

"Yeah." I couldn't quite bring myself to look at her yet. She built robots in her spare time, and I wrote fluffy things about women falling for dukes in Regency England.

"That's so cool! Why the hell didn't you tell me?"

Okay, that wasn't quite where I was expecting this to go. "Because it's romance novels, and I don't know, it's the genre that everyone makes fun of?" As Nate told me, it was garbage not worth wasting my time on. "Even though it's honestly a really interesting genre from a literary perspective. Because it's some of the only content that's created for women, by women. And it gets maligned in all of the popular press because of that."

"I feel that deeply," she said, nodding slowly.

"Great work getting overlooked because it's from a woman, yep."

"And seriously, what's kind of great about a lot of the recent romance novels is that they deal sensitively with issues like consent and trust and overcoming toxic masculinity. It's not all about bad sex writing and shirtless men on the cover. Romance novels portray what women want, because they're written from the female perspective, by women," I added.

She reached over towards me and clapped me on the shoulder. "You feel this strongly about this and you haven't told me? You have a feminist rant that you've been keeping inside all this time?"

I hadn't had a chance to go on my rant recently, and it had been building up. "Sorry, Spence."

"Don't you dare apologize for defending women's ability to create cool shit." She grinned at me, throwing her arms to the side. "But I just – how do you do something this cool and not tell me about it?"

"This cool?" Those words weren't quite making sense. I'd never had someone tell me that this was a good thing.

"Yeah! I mean, I want to read what you've written. And even if it isn't totally what I would totally read normally, I want to support you. You got picked out of all the writers in the world to ghostwrite. Shouldn't you be trumpeting this everywhere?"

I stared at her for a second. I had thought that it was going to turn into a joke. The punchline to one of

Nate's more cutting jokes. *You know Ari's going to end up a stay at home wife because she thinks she can be a romance writer, ha ha.*

"I guess – I guess that I think people would think it was a joke." And it was so much easier to share my writing with anonymous strangers than it was to think about any of my friends reading it. Especially the sex scenes. I did not want my friends reading anything I wrote that had a sex scene in it. You could kill me now.

"Are you kidding, Ari? This is a big thing." She sat back down on the couch and stared up at me, crossing her legs back into her settled position. "It's so cool. You're such a badass for doing it."

"Thanks," I said, my face flushing. "But – please don't tell the rest of the group."

"Why not?" She reached over and slung an arm around my shoulder. "Arielle, you cannot seriously think that someone is going to think less of you because you write romance novels. Honestly, that's great. And you get paid for this! I have to run around and make sure that my freshmen don't fail, and you get to sit in the apartment and write novels. That is an objectively cool thing to do."

"Thanks," I said, blushing again.

She took a sip of her coffee. "If you don't want me to tell everyone else, I won't. Because I'm not the kind of friend who would go spilling your secrets."

"You did just hold my laptop hostage," I objected, since it seemed like she was forgetting that already.

"True. But I'm not going to tell people until you're ready to tell them. Although I think you're really underselling how cool this is, Ari. You are an actual published writer."

"They pay to buy Athena Brigette's books. It's totally different," I said, picking up my own coffee.

"How different is that really? They're still paying money in order to be able to read things that you have read." She shook her head, then paused. "And I actually think I've heard of Athena Brigette."

"She has a pretty decent following." A following that would be sure to vocally express if they were disappointed with whatever I'd written. "It makes it tougher. Like if I don't live up to their expectations, they will write to the editor and let her know they think I screwed up."

Spencer shook her head again. "Sometimes I think you take the most impressive parts of yourself and hide them."

"Was that meant as a compliment?" Because it didn't sound like a compliment to me.

She tilted her head to the side and stared at me for a second. "I think so. You have lots of good parts, it's just a bad thing that you're hiding them. You sometimes don't show all of the cool things that you're actually capable of."

Like thinking about opening up your heart to another person after things ended with Nate. Being yourself and proud of yourself, despite what that asshole told you. Telling the voice in the back of your head to go screw itself, you were proud of what you'd written.

Spencer looked over and grinned at me. "And since I know you're now a published author, you're responsible for buying the coffee from now on."

Chapter 7

A week later, I stood in front of my closet and sighed. What did you wear when you needed to tell your parents to leave you alone? I needed to look cool and sophisticated enough that they would know I was a real adult, but not too sexy, so we could avoid that lecture.

In the living room, I could hear Spencer banging around, looking for something. Despite the fact that we were living in a large one bedroom, we still managed to lose things. "Do you have any idea where I stuck my quantum physics book?"

"Probably in a black hole somewhere." I grabbed a cardigan and started to button it up. Nope. Now I looked like I was dressing up as a librarian stereotype for Halloween.

"You're not funny," she called back, and I heard

the couch cushion being ripped off. "But you might be right."

"That's usually the case." I stared at myself in the mirror again, unbuttoning the cardigan. That was slightly better.

"What are you doing?" she asked, coming into my room. She leaned against the doorframe and looked at me. "Please get rid of that cardigan."

"You're not helpful," I said, turning and making sure that I looked okay from the back.

"I'm helpful because I'm telling you that it looks terrible on you. Not your color. Way too pastel."

Ugh. I turned towards her, running my fingers through my hair. "I have to have dinner with my parents tonight."

"Oh god. I'm sorry." Spencer wrapped her arms around me. "It's going to be okay. And we can go get drunk afterwards if not."

"It could be worse." I stared at myself in the mirror again. Something was still wrong. Screw it. I'd just wear jeans, and my parents could deal with it.

"Well, if you need me to fake an emergency to help you get out of the meeting, I will totally do it. I can invent something life threatening. And honestly, if I don't find this book soon, it will probably be life threatening," she said, turning back into the living room.

I snorted. "I'm pretty sure that you can survive without your quantum physics book."

"I took this class because I thought it would be a fun elective, okay? I had no idea that it was going to be so hard," she said, now opening a cabinet.

"Spence, it's literally quantum physics. Of course it's going to be hard."

"I think writing and understanding all of that stuff is hard. I don't think that physics is hard. You put some numbers into an equation, and things happen because they are logical and reasonable. With people, you never know what you're going to get." She shook her head. "I wish the world was ruled by math."

"I don't think that you actually wish that. I'm pretty sure you'd get bored of that pretty quickly," I replied, stepping into a pair of jeans.

"Maybe, but think of how much easier the world would be. Imagine group projects where everyone could be convinced with logic to do their part. It sounds like heaven." She shook her head, picking up a couch cushion again and then turning back towards me. "Go. Don't be late for dinner."

I forced a smile, reaching for my nicest jacket. "Don't worry. I won't be late and make all of this worse."

She reached over and squeezed me into a side hug before I headed off. "You're going to crush it."

I walked out of the apartment and down the street towards the middle of town. I reached the door of the restaurant and pushed it open, stepping in out of the cold outside. "I'm here with the Mack family," I said to the hostess.

"Welcome." She grabbed a menu and started walking into the restaurant. "Follow me."

I followed her through the restaurant. This was the nicest restaurant in town, a French place with high ceilings and a waterfall in the back. The waterfall was overkill, but it did mean that no one could overhear your conversations. Raleigh had told me this was the most popular place for public breakups on campus because of that.

We reached the table where my mother and father were already sitting. Both of them looked perfectly put together, my mom wearing a full face of makeup in a college town and my dad wearing a freshly pressed shirt. Of course, because appearances were the most important.

"Running a bit behind schedule today, Arielle?" my dad asked, nodding towards me as I pulled out my chair and sat down.

"It's been a busy semester." My parents didn't know half of it. I hadn't told them about ghostwriting, because they'd made it clear that they agreed with Nate. My future role was to manage communications for their chain of car dealerships, then settle down and support Nate. I wasn't going to embarrass them writing smut.

I had told them about fan fiction at one point, and my mom's immediate reply had been that I wasn't allowed to publish anything. *Don't embarrass our family that way. What if someone finds out it's you and connects it with us? Responsible adults don't do that.*

"How are your classes going?" my mom asked, finding a topic that felt like it was a safe one for us to discuss.

I swallowed, taking a sip of the water in front of me. "I have a really interesting English class this year about Jane Austen." It was one of the coolest classes that I thought the entire school offered, tracing how Jane Austen had basically invented the concept of the real romance novel. And how many of her characters were more revolutionary and had more agency that they got credit for. It was usually for sophomores, but I'd missed it in the past because of my Nate visits.

"That doesn't seem like it's going to be very practical for your career," my mom said. The waiter arrived with glasses of wine and calamari. My parents didn't like surprises, so we got the same thing every time that we went out to dinner.

"It doesn't have to be practical for my career. I want to take things that make me think. Like, classes that I actually enjoy and do well in." You only got to go to college once. I got to work for forty years. Fifty years, probably.

My mom and dad exchanged another look. "I'm not sure that we're paying for you to take fun things," my dad said, crossing his arms over his chest. "I think we're paying for you to go to college so that you can make sure that you're well prepared to get a job and work afterwards."

Yeah, he'd made that clear when he'd started only paying for my credits in communications. "I like my English classes, though," I said, reaching for a piece of calamari. My mom looked down at my nails, as though she was checking to see if I was wearing nail polish. "Half of my communications classes will be obsolete soon anyway, given how quickly social media trends change."

My mom raised an eyebrow, still looking down at my hands. I got the message, thanks. "But you will be employable if you have a communications degree. Nobody wants to hire an English major."

"That's not true." I was literally making money right now from my writing. And maybe I hadn't needed college to learn how to do that, but the English classes were helping a whole lot more than the communications ones. I wanted to learn how to think about characters and plot development, not write another case study about a General Mills tweet.

"We just want to make sure that you're in the best position for the rest of your life, Arielle." Because of course in their eyes, that was communications and following them into the family business.

Fortunately, the waiter came over to get our orders, and it gave me a chance to lean down and study my menu. My mom started to order her food, giving a full list of all of the allergies she was convinced that she had.

"I'll have a burger and fries," I said, passing the menu back.

My mom glanced over at me, her eyes narrowing. *Ladies don't order food that has to be eaten with their hands, Arielle.* "I'll have the Cobb salad," she said. "Light dressing, no blue cheese, no bacon."

The waiter nodded, picking up our menus. "So how are your friends doing?" my dad asked. He always asked, probably out of politeness, but I wasn't sure he could even list my friends' names.

"My friend Spence, my roommate, she's taking quantum physics right now and she loves it," I said. Come on, Mom. I wanted to say. Pick a fight with me about whether Spencer is going to get a job after college with her classes in quantum physics.

My mom didn't take the bait. "That's very good for her. I'm glad that she's enjoying it."

We sat in silence for a little bit longer. God, I was going to have to be the person to break the silence and get the family talking, or else this was going to be a terrible, awkward conversation. And I'd had enough of those for a lifetime already. "How is the business going?"

My dad perked right up. "Oh, it's great. Did we tell you that we're looking at a new site to expand?"

Of course this topic change worked. "In town?" I took another several pieces of calamari.

"In Pleasantview, actually," my mom said, leaning forward. We were back on safe conversational ground. I nodded. "And you know that the Kingstons are interested in partnering with us on the next one."

Oh. I should have known that that was coming. I wasn't sure that I could have avoided it for much longer. *Arielle needs to get over herself and get back together with Nate. She's being a silly girl.*

My mom cleared her throat and looked from my dad back to me. "I assume that you have heard that Nate has been seeing someone."

The blood rushed to my ears, and I closed my eyes for a second. I didn't want to hear about it.

"But his parents assured us that it's not serious," she continued. "He's still very upset about what happened between the two of you. If you could just bring yourself to apologize – "

"Apologize?" Were they kidding me? They thought that I would ever go back to that piece of shit? "What the hell is supposed to mean?"

My mom's eyes widened, and she glanced over at my dad. "What we mean to say is that you and Nate were always so perfect together. We don't want a little bit of college drama to get in the way."

"It wasn't college drama, Mom." College drama was kissing someone else at a party. College drama would have been getting drunk and throwing up. It hadn't been college drama.

"Then tell us what it was, Arielle," my dad said,

resting his forearms on the table and leaning towards me. "You know that we had always planned to leave the business to you and Nate, and you chose to throw all that away."

"You know that the two of you were great together," my mom added. "And our families are so close."

I stared at them. *College drama.*

I hadn't told them the whole truth, because I didn't want to throw that bomb into our family. But if they were going to sit here, I wasn't taking it any more. "I broke up with Nate because he cheated on me. Multiple times."

Go on. I told you. Tell me you understand.

My mom and dad looked at each other. They had to get it now. They'd never think that Nate would cheat, but now they knew.

For a second, I thought my mom's face had softened, but she shook her head. "Nate would never have done that. He's a good boy from a good family."

"His family has nothing to do with this!" I swallowed. If I got too emotional, my dad would just ignore me. "I'm telling you. He cheated. I'm not going to be with someone who cheats. And he never supported what I wanted to do."

"Never supported what you wanted to do?" My dad leaned forward towards me. "Nate has his head on straight, unlike you, Arielle. He knows that his job is to take over the business. He's studying business and making good contacts in college, not wasting his time reading about Jane Austen."

My mom leaned towards me. "And there's just no way that he cheated. It sounds like you're letting jealousy get the better of you, Arielle. It's very unbecoming."

Were they kidding me? I stared at them. Their only child was telling them how badly Nate had hurt her, and they were jumping to defend him instead of me? "I know he cheated. He didn't even bother to hide it. I'm not tolerating that."

"Sometimes you have to be the bigger person, Arielle," my mom said, giving me a look. "You know that girls throw themselves at Nate all the time, because he's such a wonderful young man."

Oh, so we were slut shaming now? The toxic masculinity in here was choking me. "He's not a wonderful young man. He throws himself at girls because he can't keep it in his pants, and he never respected me."

"Arielle! We don't use that kind of language," my dad said, pointing a fork at me. "You know the Kingstons are our closest friends."

So we were going to put our family friends above our actual family. I had too much self-respect to put up with this. I looked around the restaurant, then stood back up. "I'm going to leave now."

And with that, I turned and started the walk out of the restaurant and back towards my home.

Chapter 8

"How did it go?" Spence took one look at my face as I walked through the door. "Oh shit. Not good."

"It was horrible. I finally told them what happened with Nate, and they didn't believe me," My vision even seemed to blur as I said it, my heart pounding. I had finally said it, and my parents had still sided with Nate.

"Oh, screw those assholes. Do you need a hug?" Spence stared at me for another second. "No, you don't look like you want a hug."

"They think that I'm being irrational." My voice rose again, and I clenched my fist. They'd actually sided with Nate.

"They're the ones being irrational if they think that!" She reached over and passed me one of the drinks she had on the side. I grabbed it, squeezing the can to take out my frustration. "He was an asshole. And we are leaving him in the past."

I wouldn't take him back if I could. The longer I was away from it, the more it hurt. Instead of my parents rallying around me, they assumed I was throwing everything away.

And my parents still made it all about them. That they were upset that I was giving this up. That I should have been more considerate because they were business partners. That my life and my happiness didn't seem to fit into what they had already planned for me.

"I want tequila," I said, turning towards Spencer. It might not be healthy, but I could have healthy coping tomorrow. "That's what I need right now."

"If what you need is to get drunk and forget the world tonight, I'm not going to stand in your way," she said, opening up one of the cabinets and starting to rummage around. "Do you want the cheap stuff or the really cheap stuff?"

Today was going to be a day for really cheap stuff. For the tequila that was going to burn going down and probably be even worse coming up. But I wasn't going to think about that for now. I was going to go out, and I was going to dance. I poured some tequila into an orange juice glass, and Spencer raised an eyebrow. "Easy there, cowboy."

"Let's go," I said, grabbing my jacket and nodding towards the door. "It's time to go out."

She raised an eyebrow, as though she wanted to make sure that I wanted to go out and not talk about this. I knew that technically, this wasn't the healthiest reaction. That I should probably be having deep conversations with someone about my feelings. But fuck it. It was what I wanted right now.

Spencer grabbed her jacket and followed me out of the apartment and down the block towards the bar. The bouncer nodded towards us and stamped our hands as we reached the door.

"Have I mentioned how excited I am that I don't have to use a fake any more?" Spence said as we walked into the bar. "I was always worried that someone was going to look too closely at it and realize what it was."

"You could have tried getting a slightly nicer fake." Nate had gotten me my fake ID from one of his well-connected friends during freshman year, after he'd exploded on me because I wasn't able to go out to bars with the rest of his friend group. It was the only thing he'd given me that I'd kept after the breakup.

The single good thing from all those years of dating was literally fake. Thanks for the irony, world.

I started banging my head to the music as soon as we got in, and Spencer doubled over laughing. "You really can't dance, Arielle."

We reached the table that Raleigh and Mason had already snagged at the back. "I heard it was an emergency going out session tonight," Raleigh shouted towards me, standing up and giving me a half hug.

"I don't want to talk about it," I shouted back over the music. "I am just here to have fun!"

"Was that what you called that attempting to dance out there?" Mason asked, and Raleigh elbowed him in the side.

"What did I miss?" Lucas came up to the table and sat down across from me, glancing around the table. "What called for the emergency party tonight?"

"Arielle had dinner with her parents." Raleigh mouthed towards Lucas.

"Shut up!" I snapped, more loudly than I thought. Everyone at the table turned to look at me. I swallowed. "I don't want to talk about it, okay? It's over." Raleigh and Spencer knew the story. That was enough. I wasn't going to have to explain it again. I wanted to forget it for now. I needed to forget it for now.

"Ari." Spencer looked over at me, putting her hand on my arm.

"I'm going to dance." I stood up from the table, shoving in my chair. I was not in the mood for a pity party, all my friends sitting around and telling me how brave I was. I was going to dance.

I was going to take myself back. Back from the person my parents thought I had to be. Back from the person that I had tried and failed to be. Back to being myself.

And with that, I stormed away from the table, right to the middle of the dance floor.

The song ended, and the opening beats of *Dancing on My Own* rang out through the whole bar. This was my shit right here. The music started to swell, and I closed my eyes. This was what I needed right here. "I'm in the corner, watching you kiss her!" I belted out, jumping up and down in the middle of the floor.

"I'm just dancing on my own!" I screamed as the last line finished. The song transitioned into the next beat, and I closed my eyes.

I'll keep dancing on my own.

"Ari?" Lucas was standing in front of me, staring at me. He reached out a hand towards me. "Are you okay?"

I was okay. I just needed to take out all of my rage on the dance floor. "I'm dancing!" I shouted back, gesturing towards the dance floor. It had gotten more and more crowded. "Don't be Spencer and tell me that my dancing looks like a malfunctioning robot."

He ran a hand through his hair. "Not that – just, like, are you okay?"

It was okay now. Because I would listen to Robyn and scream along. To finally celebrate. Because when Nate and I had broken up, I was sad. Heartbroken. Because it was such a betrayal, destroying everything I thought I wanted. Maybe I had never loved him from the beginning, because it had been something that my parents had wanted. Not me.

And now, I wanted to have a breakup. A real breakup. Where I got to be angry about the fact that he was a little piece of shit who took all those years of my life.

And I was going to drink cheap tequila, and I was going to go out to clubs, and I was going to sing my heart out at the top of my lungs. I was going to feel alive again.

I looked at him and nodded. "I'm okay. But I need to dance."

Lucas recognized this was a serious demand. He stood in front of me and started to wave his hands back and forth in the air.

The rest of the group came to join us after the next song, Spencer reaching around and giving me a side hug. "You've got this, Arielle," she whispered in my ear.

An hour later, Spencer headed out with Luisa, and it was down to me, Raleigh, and Lucas. The music started to shift to closing time, and Raleigh reached over to me. "Okay, Cinderella. Time for you to go to bed and leave the ball."

Raleigh passed Lucas my coat, and I stuck my tongue out at her. I was totally capable. "I'm not Cinderella. She has a prince. I Don't have a prince. And I don't need a prince."

"Right," Lucas said, looking down towards me and nodding slightly. "You don't need a prince." The corner of his mouth tweaked up, almost like he was making fun of me. He turned towards Raleigh. "I'll make sure that she gets home."

I didn't need him to do that, but my traitor of a friend nodded. "Thanks, Lucas," Raleigh said. "I'll see you tomorrow, Ari."

I wanted to stick my tongue out at her, but Lucas would definitely make fun of me for that.

"Can you walk in a straight line?" Lucas asked. I started to take a step and tottered on my shoes. Maybe they were Spencer's shoes. "Oops," he said, reaching out his hand and steadying my arm. "Apparently not."

"It's not that I'm drunk," I said, even though I could tell that was a little bit true. Now that the rage had worn off, I was feeling slightly tipsy. "It's Spencer's shoes."

"It's just the shoes?" Lucas asked, raising an eyebrow as we left the bar and started the walk towards my apartment.

"Maybe not just the shoes," I admitted. "I drank a lot of really cheap tequila earlier. Not just the cheap tequila, but the cheap cheap stuff. It's the tequila when you're having a bad night, you know? When you have a bad day, and then you have that really bad tequila, it makes it good again. Spencer says it's an overflow error. That when you have so much bad in the world, it becomes an overflow error and then turns into something really good."

His hand reached back out towards my arm

again, steadying me. "I'm impressed that anyone outside of the comp sci department knows what an overflow error is."

"This is why I have Spencer," I said. "She's really, really smart."

"So does it make me really smart because I also know what it is?" he asked, holding out a hand to stop me at a crosswalk.

I shook my head. "You're smart, but you aren't taking quantum physics for fun, so you're not really really smart."

He laughed, a laugh that seemed to echo around the street. "If I had known that that was what you were looking for, maybe I would have registered for it this semester."

"Maybe," I replied, pulling my coat tighter around me.

We reached our apartment. Lucas looked down at me, and then at my pockets. "Can you get your keys out? Because no offense, but you're quite drunk."

That might be true, but I wasn't going to admit it. "I'm like, little drunk. Not big drunk."

"The fact that you just described it as little drunk means that you are in fact big drunk," he replied. He held out his hand. "Keys, please."

I fished them out of my pocket and dropped them in his hand, and he unlocked the door. He held his hand behind my back as I walked up the steps towards my apartment, his hand barely brushing my back.

He unlocked the door and held it open for me. We walked up the few stairs towards the apartment, and he unlocked the inside door, too. "After you."

"This is my apartment. I know what I'm doing," I said, turning towards him and crossing my arms.

"I know. I just want to make sure that you get home safely, okay?" he said, watching me from the doorway.

"It's good," I said finally. I paused for a second. "But I'm going to sleep on the couch tonight." Spencer was probably asleep already. She was going to kill me if I woke her up. Or if she was sleeping naked and Lucas came into the room.

Before Lucas could say anything, I walked over to the couch and pulled one of the blankets up around me. He ran a hand through his hair. "I wanted to ask you something. And I mean, it's time sensitive, or I would obviously wait until I wasn't sure that you were drunk."

"I'm not big drunk. I'm little drunk."

He snorted. "Right. Little drunk. Do you want to have brunch with me and Mason and Raleigh tomorrow? My parents are in town. And you should invite Spencer, too, because my parents love a good hangover brunch with all my friends."

Oh. If I was with Lucas's parents, I couldn't be with mine. That was a good idea. "Okay," I said, snuggling deeper into the blanket. "But I like bagels. And bacon. So please have those."

He laughed again, his voice echoing around the room. "There can be bagels. And bacon. But if you change your mind when you wake up, just text me, okay?"

"Okay." Bagels and bacon with friends. Perfect.

Lucas reached down and squeezed my shoulder. "Good night, Arielle." And that was the last thing that I heard before I drifted off to sleep.

Chapter 9

"You look like shit."

I blinked twice, staring up at Spencer, who was standing in front of me holding out a mug of coffee. I was sitting on the couch wrapped in blankets. And my clothes from last night. Great. Rookie mistake. "What did we do last night?"

She held the coffee mug towards me, and I took it, wrapping both of my hands around it. It was nice and warm. "You really impressed the entire city with how well you can dance," she replied. "It was like watching one of my robots malfunction."

"Oh god. The really cheap tequila strikes again," I said.

She nodded. "Wise words. That stuff is terrible."

"You let me drink it," I protested. Wasn't the point of best friends to save you from yourself?

"You grabbed an orange juice cup and filled it up

before I had a chance to stop you," she shot back. "Drink your coffee."

My jacket was neatly hung up over one of the chairs at the dining room table, my keys on the middle of the table. My phone was even plugged in, next to a glass of water and aspirin. "Seriously, Spence? You're the best."

"I wish I could take credit, but this was all Lucas," she said, shaking her head. "He brought you back here, and I think he was quite worried that you were going to have a hangover this morning."

"He's not wrong," I said, reaching for the water and taking a giant gulp of it. "I feel like shit."

I reached for my phone. There was a text on the front screen. *Hey, it's Lucas. Hope you're feeling better.*

Thanks for bringing me home last night, and for the aspirin, I texted back. I didn't want someone to have to take care of me, but I wasn't going to be petty enough to not say thank you for it.

You were in a pretty rough spot, he texted back. *You explained overflow errors to me.*

I groaned and sunk my head into my hands. "What's wrong?" Spencer asked, sipping her coffee and smirking at me. She was enjoying this too much.

"I explained computer science to Lucas last night. How drunk was I?"

She snorted. "I hope you know that I would have paid money to see that."

And I might have paid money to have not done

that. *I'm sorry,* I texted back. *I'm sure it was a good way to explain them though.*

I'm not sure that you remember this, but I invited you and Spencer to brunch this morning, he texted. "Apparently we're invited to brunch with Lucas's parents," I said, looking up at Spencer.

"I would be down, but I have to lead a tutoring session bright and early on a Sunday morning. This is how we haze the new majors." She stood up and stretched, then nodded towards my coffee. "Drink up. If you've got brunch plans, you need to make yourself look presentable a whole lot faster than we were expecting."

Ugh, that was right. I cradled the coffee cup in my hands, sniffing the steam. "Give me five."

An hour and a half later, I left the apartment and headed towards the middle of town. I stopped in front of the hotel, checking down to make sure that my coat wasn't covered in salt. "Hey," Lucas said, walking up from the other direction and nodding towards me.

"Of course," I said. Part of my brain was freaking out a little about seeing Lucas here, about what I might have said the night before. I was sure that it wasn't anything too embarrassing. Then again, it had been the really cheap tequila.

"Mason canceled on me this morning because he was hungover, Spence texted that she was at tutoring, and I didn't want to have to do this alone," he said, looking away from me and towards the hotel. The wind lifted his hair, and he shoved his hands deeper into his pockets.

"Wait, so it's just me? I thought it was going to be everyone." Not where it was weird and I was the token friend who was showing up alongside everybody else.

He sighed again. "Mason says he's too hungover. Which I understand, but I'm still annoyed at them. Mason and my dad are best friends."

Well, this was quickly turning more and more awkward. I followed him into the restaurant. There was a couple standing in front of the host stand. They glanced over towards us, and then the woman started waving her arms as though she was helping a plane land. "Lucas! And Lucas's new friend! Hello!"

"And those are my parents," Lucas muttered under his breath.

I wasn't sure I could have found a bigger difference to my parents if I had tried. Lucas's parents looked exactly like friends of my parents', but as soon as I walked over, his mom turned and beamed at me. "Hi! I'm Lilly. Can I give you a hug? I'm a hugger."

I just nodded, and she wrapped me into a giant hug. "We're always so happy to meet Lucas's friends! And you are?"

"Arielle," I said, taking a step back. "Arielle Mack."

"Like the truck?" His dad turned towards me,

grinning. He stared at my face for a second, his face falling. "I'm guessing you've heard that joke before."

"If it's a joke about cheeseburgers, trucks, or computers, I've heard it before," I said. Hopefully that didn't sound snarky. I didn't want to be snarky to someone else's parents, not when they were going to buy me breakfast.

"Return of the Mack!" His dad pointed two finger guns at me, then clapped his hands together. I stared at him for a second, and he eventually shook his head. "No? That reference is too old for you?"

"Dad. Every reference that you make is too old," Lucas said, looking down towards the floor.

"Let's find our seats, shall we? It's time for some pancakes," his mom said. I followed the group to the back of the restaurant. We arrived at a table for four, and I pulled out my chair.

Lucas reached around and got there before I could, pulling it out for me to sit down. I glanced at him for a second, then sat down. Maybe it was a weird family thing, where it was part of how they tried to be nice to each other. Unnecessary chivalry and things.

"So how are classes going?" Lucas's dad asked as we scooted in. The waiter had already left a basket of rolls in the middle of the table, and Lucas's mom put one on her plate and one on mine.

"They're good." Lucas stared at his coffee.

"Are they too stressful?" his mom asked, turning

towards him. "Are you finding them interesting and a good challenge or overwhelming?"

"They're fine," Lucas replied, not meeting her eyes.

"It's always okay to take time off if you need it. You know that, right?" she asked, still trying to make eye contact with him. Lucas reached towards the cup of coffee that had been set down in front of him and stared at it.

Before the silence could get awkward, she turned towards me. "So what do you do, Arielle?"

Lucas was looking down at his food, poking it with his fork. Actually, poking was the wrong verb. He was stabbing his food with his fork, as though there was no other way to show it.His shoulders were tense. I wanted to reach over and pull him into a hug.

"I'm an English major," I said. Technically also a communications major, but there was no point in mentioning the boring one.

"So what are you planning to do after college?" She caught my eye, then shook her head. "You don't have to answer that! I know that I always hated that question."

"She still hates that question," Lucas's dad said, reaching over and rustling her hair.

I swallowed. I knew what I wanted to do, but I didn't know how I was going to do it. "I don't know yet. I'm considering a lot of things." Living off my writing, but I wasn't sure how yet.

"Well, no need to have all the answers in your twenties!" Lucas's dad chimed in.

"And the only thing that matters is that you're happy," his mom finished, beaming at me. The waiter came around with more coffee, and she gestured towards my cup. "Do you need more coffee? You look like you need more coffee."

The waiter came by to take our orders. This time, I was going to get the food that I wanted to eat for brunch. "The hungry person special, please, with extra bacon."

Lucas's mom looked over at me. "You're tempting me to change my order to that from French toast!"

"And she never gets anything other than pancakes or French toast," Lucas's dad said, leaning towards me. "I took her out to a Michelin-starred brunch place once as a special treat, and she told them all she wanted were pancakes."

"There's nothing wrong with having a passion and going for it!" She grinned at her husband, then looked up at the waiter. "Pancakes for me. But can I get a side of French toast too?"

Lucas looked like he wanted to sink into the floor. "I'll do the hungry person too."

"So," his mom said as the waiter left the table. "Did you hear that Max was admitted to Stanford Law?"

"Big surprise," Lucas mumbled, reaching for the

bread in the middle of the table. "He was always the best at everything."

"It doesn't matter if you're technically the best or not as long as you love what you do!" His mom looked at him, the corners of her eyes soft. "That's what matters to us."

Lucas looked away, and I could almost imagine what was going through his head. *Yeah, that's what you say to the loser kid. Good attempt.*

"Lucas is very successful at school," I said, suddenly feeling like I had to say something. "He's one of the top students in the computer science department. He even explained computer science to all of us last night. Overflow errors."

"That's awesome!" His dad's face lit up like I'd told him that Lucas had single-handedly cured cancer. "Computer science is a really difficult field, and you should be so proud of yourself for all the hard work that you've put into it."

"Dad, seriously," Lucas said. His jaw jumped as he chewed a piece of scrambled egg.

His parents exchanged looks between the two of them, and then his mom turned back towards me. "Arielle, has Lucas told you about our dog at home?"

"Oh, you have to hear this," his dad said, leaning forward.

And with that, the conversation was off, his mom excitedly describing how their dog had become an escape artist and convinced the neighbors that it was a stray that needed to be fed. I lost myself in the story, and even Lucas started to laugh as we got into it.

Almost an hour later, we finished brunch and paid the bill. "It was lovely to meet you, Arielle," his mom said, reaching over and giving me a huge hug. "And next time, maybe you can drag Raleigh and Mason out too! We miss those two."

"Yep. I'll do that," Lucas said, his voice strained. "Come on, Ari. I can give you a ride home."

That didn't sound like it was a friendly offer so much as a plea. "It's great to meet you," I said, nodding towards his parents. "Thanks for brunch."

They did something that could have been a wave, and I followed Lucas off towards his car. "That was more fun than I expected," I said as he pulled away.

"They're a lot," he said, his voice quiet.

I glanced over at him, trying to read his expression. They were a lot, I wanted to say, but that was a good thing. They were explosions of color, while my parents were black and white.

But he didn't seem to want to talk, and we sat in silence until he pulled up in front of my apartment. "Thanks for coming," he said as I unbuckled my seatbelt.

I looked over at him, waiting for him to say something more. But he didn't, so I just nodded. "Thanks for breakfast."

As I walked back into the apartment, I spotted Spencer sitting on the couch. She looked up at me, giving me an unnaturally wide grin. "How was brunch with the wolf pack?"

"Please never call them that again," I said, unzipping my coat and hanging it on the back of a chair.

"It's an accurate description, right? Because there were a lot of people named Wolf. I make the best jokes."

"Or there's a reason that you're a scientist and not a stand up comedian," I said, sitting down and starting to take off my shoes

"Yeah, I couldn't deal with the heckling," she said, crossing her legs underneath her and tilting her head to the side. "Was it you and Mason and Raleigh? I'm sad I missed it."

"Just me." I walked over to the coffeemaker that Spence had pulled out and poured myself another cup. I had already had coffee at breakfast, sure, but also, I had a hangover coming on. I had to get through my work today as a functional human, and that was going to require coffee.

She stared at me for a second. "Seriously? Just you meeting his parents?"

"It wasn't like that. I was just the only person who could make it. And I don't like him like that," I said again. The problem was that it was becoming less and less convincing to me every time I said it.

God, and now I was thinking about how he looked when we were driving back, when his hair was blown by the wind outside of the restaurant. When he had looked so handsome that I had wanted to reach over and put my hand on his back.

"Oh, come on. You were all sad because he didn't kiss you the other week. You do like him like that, and I know that you think things with Nate just ended, but you're pushing him away for no reason," Spencer said.

There was a side of my brain that was screaming at me right now. That I had been hurt so many times before, and I wasn't ready for another round of that. That I just wanted things to be fine and normal and easy for a while.

But that wasn't going to happen. He liked me like that. And I knew it. I knew it. Because I might be hesitant about things, but I wasn't blind. I wasn't an idiot.

Maybe in two years he would be the right guy. He was smart, funny, and nice. Sometimes a little bit annoying, sometimes a little bit of a stone wall, but it wasn't like there was a perfect person. He was real.

I didn't want Nate back, but he was still hovering in my mind. When I was with Nate, I'd lost Arielle. I'd turned into a person who I didn't know, who had been willing to give up all of her hopes and dreams for someone else. I wanted to keep being myself, not fall back into just being someone's girlfriend. I didn't know if I could do that and date Lucas.

I closed my eyes for a second and took a long drink of my coffee. "I know."

. . .

IT WAS another gray day on campus. I grabbed my backpack and headed towards the student center. I had agreed to work on a communications project with Lilith, one of the girls in my class, and I was rapidly regretting that decision.

Our new project was going to have to be standing up in front of the classroom and talking through a communications problem, followed by suggestions for how to handle it in the future. I reached the table where Lilith was already sitting, staring down at her book.

Lilith and I had been in communications classes together since freshman year, and she was one of the few people I genuinely liked in that major. Most of the people were there to get jobs, and they were not fun. Lilith, on the other hand, had done interpretive dance in one of our early classes, because she told me it was a good way to get people to think. She was fun.

"Hey," I said, sitting down across from her. "Any luck getting this started so far?"

She looked up, pushing a piece of hair out of her face. "Why did we get this prompt? You are a fashion brand where your founder has recently stated that women who weigh more than a hundred twenty pounds should not buy your brand. You are the head of corporate communications and need to figure out your response strategy."

"Fire the CEO?" I suggested. "Because if they're going to be that terrible of a person, then we shouldn't have them as a CEO." That was the only appropriate response to that. If someone said that to me, Spencer would have punched them. Or designed a killer robot to stalk them around campus.

"That's what I want to say," she said, pulling the prompt that we'd gotten out of her binder. "Like, why would you want to have a terrible person as CEO? Can't you just get rid of them?"

"I don't think that we would pass the class if we suggested that, but I would much, much rather do that than come up with a response strategy," I said, looking down at the paper in front of us again. It was a smug white guy in the photo on the brief. "Like, doesn't this guy just look like he's going to be an asshole?"

She followed my gaze down to the paper and then nodded. "He looks like he kicks puppies. Do you think we'd pass if we just suggested quitting and moving to a new company, because we wanted to make sure that we were working for a company that matches what we believe in?"

If only. "Probably not. I think the point of this class is learning how to deal with situations where people are acting like terrible humans." Honestly, that felt like the whole major sometimes. All of the classes were about apologizing without apologizing.

"I hate this major. This whole project sucks," she said, taking a drink out of her water bottle.

"Okay," I said, clearing my throat and looking back down at the prompt. "So I think that we should deny that this ever happened." It was often easier to deny things than to try to explain them away. Gaslighting our way into PR success.

"You think that we have to deny it?" she asked, turning and looking at me. "But it's obvious. Everyone knows that he said it. We can't just pretend that it never happened."

"But we can't talk about it, because that's going to make it worse," I argued back. "The more we talk about it, the worse we're going to make it seem. Just ignore it and let it blow over. Like, if there's a consumer boycott, it's not going to last that long."

She stared at me for a second, tapping her pencil on the table some more. "This doesn't seem like a good idea. None of this seems like a good idea. I mean, in your life, you don't just ignore people who say things like this."

"When I'm the one insulted?" I swallowed. I had never confronted Nate, and that had been okay. I had told him over the phone, and then I had just blocked his number and left. Because there was nothing more than I could have from him. "That has worked in the past. You just become a bigger person and you move on."

Lilith crossed her arms and tilted her head to the

side. "First of all, I don't think that that's right at all, but also, in that case, you were the one insulted. You had to put up with it because you didn't want to face it. But if that person was a clothing brand, you'd never shop there again."

"I mean, I never went back to the person," I added, in case there were any questions about that. Not that I had managed to confront him or my parents about what had happened, but I hadn't gone back to him.

"I think you just proved my point for me," she said.

Right, yeah. I was supposed to be focused on the schoolwork here. "Maybe we can look up the thing that this case is based on, and then we can talk through what we think that we should do next?" she said.

I swallowed. "Yeah. That sounds like a good idea."

She nodded towards me. "And I think you'll realize why denial might not be the best strategy for this one."

Was Lilith turning into Spencer and giving me life advice? I nodded. I deserved that. I was pretty sure that she was right. But sometimes it felt like the right idea in the short term.

Part of communications was learning how to make sure that nothing got blown out of proportion. I wasn't doing a good job of that. In class or in my personal life, apparently.

And just like that, I looked up from where I was sitting and tried to focus on my classwork.

Lucas was sitting on the other side of the student center. He looked like he was studying too, a bunch of people with books and computers around them. One of the girls in the group said something to him, and he threw his head back and laughed. She leaned forward, like she was going to put her hand on his arm.

My heart started pounding, and I could feel my face flushing from all the way over here.

"What are you thinking?" Lilith asked, looking up.

"Nothing." I wasn't going to admit that I was thinking about a guy instead of focusing on the much more important work in front of us. I needed a quick save. "Actually, embarrassing, but your top. It's not from the same store that we're talking about, is it?"

She looked down at her top and then started laughing. "Oh my god. You're right. I better remember not to wear this to class."

"Or you should remember to, because it proves that they fixed the situation eventually." Deep breath. Focusing again.

She shook her head. "Okay. Let's focus again. This."

I closed my eyes for a second, blocking out the thought of Lucas. "Right. I'm focusing."

Chapter 10

My cell phone rang, and I stared down at it for a second. It was a New York number, but not one I knew.

I let the phone keep ringing, turning back towards my computer. I propped my feet up on the coffee table in front of me, reaching for the cup of tea that I had been nursing earlier. It was getting cold now.

My phone beeped twice, and I looked over to see a text. *Call me back. This is Margaret Siskind from your publisher.*

I didn't want to talk about *The Lord Who Loved Me* right now. I was entirely behind on that, but I wasn't going to think about that. I'd come up with an excuse. And then I was going to actually make some progress on it this weekend. But I couldn't ignore my publisher when she was calling.

I picked up my phone and dialed the number

again. "Hi, this is Arielle Mack, returning a call from Margaret Siskind?"

"This is she," the voice on the other end said. It was clipped and a little bit brisk, and I blinked a couple of times. Usually when my editor called, it was all smiles, telling me how much I'd grown as a writer. "I assume you've heard the news."

"What news?" I asked. I had the sinking feeling of being really far behind something.

"Emma quit," Margaret said.

"Emma left?" Emma had been my editor forever. She was the kind of person where I wanted to go have a cup of tea with her and talk about books. She lived in a house in the countryside with chintz seats and big overstuffed couches and reading nooks. She rescued animals and took filtered pictures for Instagram. Being Emma was my life goal, in other words.

She was supportive, too. When I had gotten bad reviews on one of the novels, she'd give me a pep talk about how I needed to make sure that I believed in myself first. Everyone got bad reviews, even Michelle Obama.

"I'm surprised that you didn't get a call from her. I heard she called everyone five times just to be sure that she didn't miss anyone," Margaret said.

That sounded more like the Emma I knew. "So?" I asked, my voice small. "What does this mean for the Athena Brigette series?"

"For all of her ghostwriters, you mean? Because I

can tell you that Athena Brigette hasn't typed a word in the past five years, unless it's her online banking password to check her royalty checks," Margaret replied.

I shut my eyes for a second. Emma had always made a point to call us authors, even if we were writing under someone else's name. It was a rite of passage for a lot of romance writers, and it wasn't any different than anyone else publishing under a pen name. "Yes, the ghostwriters," I said.

"Well, I'm your new editor."

My heart felt like it dropped through the floor. I would have yelled at myself for putting that into one of my books, but that was how it felt to me. Like the whole world had stopped for a second so that I could process the news. "*You're* my new editor?"

"That's right. I wanted to call you, introduce myself, and make sure that we're on the same page about how we're going to turn the ship around," she said. "I don't want this to be a surprise."

"Turn the ship around?" I repeated. My brain could only take so much bad news at a time.

There was a pause. "Had Emma not told you about the situation? Our sales numbers have been dramatically down. It's getting eaten alive by every other Regency and Regency-lite romance out there." I heard her tapping a pencil on the other side of the phone line.

That couldn't be the case. We'd done better and

better with the writing for the last ones. And I thought that some of mine had been pretty good.

"So," she continued, clearing her throat, "we're going to need to hustle and fix that sales slump with the next book."

"What do you mean?" I asked. My voice was softer and smaller than I had expected. I wanted to sound more authoritative, damn it. I wanted to be the person who stood up for all of the writing that we had done. Because it was good, damn it. Emma had always said so.

"The reviews haven't been great on the series, and I'm looking for a next book that's going to make Athena Brigette the next romance sensation. We need it to save the series," she said. "This is serious."

I stared at my laptop, at the copy of *The Lord Who Loved Me* that was barely written in my minimized documents. I was working on it. I was seriously working on it. "Of course." I swallowed again. "I can definitely do that."

Romance was hard. I had to get the reader to fall in love with my characters alongside me, and then I had to make sure that they felt it when things went wrong. It was easy to write bad romance, sure. But it was really, really hard to write good romance.

"Great. I'm looking forward to reading what you get me." There was a pause, and the sound of more pencil tapping. "And I know this is different from how Emma did things, but I am strict on deadlines. I want a first draft that can be turned around with minimal edits. If we can't agree on that as our standard, we're not a good author and editor match."

Unfortunately, I knew exactly what that meant. That meant that I would get fired if I didn't hit her deadlines exactly.

I didn't want to have to get another job, but I couldn't ask my parents for money. That had been clear enough with all of the things that they had said about my writing and about Nate and about my life. "Of course," I said, swallowing again. I couldn't let my editor think that I was going to have some kind of breakdown.

"Great." Her voice wasn't unfriendly, just brisk. "I expect to see your draft in my inbox in four weeks sharp. I look forward to it."

Four weeks. God, I knew that I had to get moving on the book, but I had assumed that I was going to get at least one extension. Emma always gave me extensions.

I could have told Emma that I was finishing college and going through things, and she would have talked with me about it. She would have encouraged me to write through my feelings and to find what I could from the experience. And she would have told me I was going to be okay.

"Thanks," I said, swallowing and hanging up the phone. I stared at my computer, blinking. I was pretty sure there was a tear forming in one of my eyes, more from frustration than from sadness. Emma had left, and my job was threatening to vanish along with her.

Spencer pushed open the door, a bag of groceries over one of her arms. She stared at me for a second. "You okay, Ari? You look sad."

I had to pull off a miracle in the next few weeks. If I got fired, I'd have to figure out how to pay for school on my own. Getting fired would be a big nope to my long term dream of living off my writing. If I couldn't even do it when I was in college and had a great gig, how was I going to do it forever?

But I couldn't tell Spencer that. I wasn't ready to talk about it yet. She'd be too supportive and try to help. I swallowed. "Yeah. I'm fine."

Chapter 11

"How's it going?" Spencer asked as I walked into the apartment.

"I'm so tired." If it wasn't the communications project with Lilith, it was finishing *The Lord who Loved Me*. It hadn't been going as well as I had expected. I was suffering from writer's block. Or not block, exactly, but something that was close enough to it. I couldn't get the words to come out right and make sure that it made a story.

"What's so stressful about this particular communications project?" she asked, sticking a book into her backpack. She was heading out for another of her tutoring sessions.

"I – " I swallowed, not totally believing that I was going to say this out loud. "I'm wondering if I should drop the class."

"Drop the class senior year?" she asked, turning

towards me and tilting her head towards the side. "Isn't it required for the major?"

I sighed. "I'm thinking maybe I should just drop the major."

She narrowed her eyes, looking straight at me. "You totally should if you want to. But on the other hand, all you have to do is pass this one class and you have a second major."

I stared at her for a second, then the words that were bubbling up in the back of my head started to come out. "It was Nate's idea that I take the communications major."

She stared at me for a second. "He who must not be named is making another appearance?"

I nodded. "I mean – "

"Wait, I thought communications was your idea. Because you wanted to make sure that you had something that was going to be a major that you thought you could get a job with. Because you were worried about not having a job with English," she finished.

"I hate it." Oh god, the words were finally starting to come out. "Nate told me that I needed to make sure that I could support the family business later on. And so I should learn something useful. Like communications."

"And you listened to him?" she asked, her eyebrows flying up.

"I know!" I swallowed. "But maybe he had a point. I hate it, but it is practical."

Spencer tilted her head, staring at me for a second. "I mean, maybe. I definitely don't want to say that that asshole could be right about anything. But maybe you want to do something that communications will help with?"

"Maybe." I just couldn't get past the sense of it being wrong. It was my senior year and I didn't even want to go to class. It was that far gone.

"Unsolicited advice, but get through this presentation and then think about it. It could just be presentation stress, you know?" She zipped up her backpack, standing up. "Want to walk to campus with me?"

I nodded, grabbing my bag. "So how is everything else going?" she asked as we started the walk. "And if you're going to tell me something about Lucas, I don't want to hear it. Because you need to have a more multidimensional personality than that."

"Shut up. At least he didn't propose to me in a tutoring session," I replied.

"You were supposed to never talk about that again. You're lucky that I love living with you, or I don't know if I'd put up with this shit," she said, shaking her head.

We reached where the path diverged. Spencer pulled me into a side hug, and then she headed off towards her next class. I took another deep breath and walked into the communications building. Senior seminar was a huge class, with a hundred people in our section alone, and I walked by twenty rows of seats until I found Lilith.

"How are you feeling?" Lilith asked as I slipped into the seat next to her.

"Honestly, nervous." I didn't even want to be in this major. Spencer was right, though. This could all just be nerves about the presentation.

"As long as Professor Jenkins doesn't totally destroy us, we'll be fine," she said, reaching over and giving me a tiny bump in the arm. "You know that he was on the warpath yesterday."

Professor Jenkins had worked as a communications consultant for a long time. When he retired, he became a professor because he thought that college students were too coddled and special snowflakes. He let us know his opinion on that all the time.

"Let's get started," he said from the front of the room, looking around at all of us. "I'd like to see a few of you learn how to pay attention to the time."

A student tried to push through the door thirty seconds late, and he turned. "You can sit in the hallway today and hope that your group isn't called. I don't accept tardiness in my class."

The student stared at him for a second, opening and closing his mouth. "Yes?" Professor Jenkins said. "If you call yourself a communications major, you should be able to communicate with me."

Rumor has it that the school had wanted to cut him from the staff because there were so many complaints. Of course, the state had budget cuts, and Professor Jenkins offered to work for a dollar a year. A bunch of people who also believed that he was right about us all being too delicate threatened to not donate to the college. So the college had kept him.

He rapped his knuckles against the table in the front. "As I've said previously, every group in this class will present their proposed response to a challenging corporate situation. The class will vote on the best and worst responses, and from that, I will grade all of you on a curve. In the real world, your company isn't going to get participation credit, so you're not going to get it either. If you're in last place in the class voting, you're going to fail the assignment. Hopefully that isn't too difficult for you to understand."

Lilith and I exchanged glances. Of course. Honestly, it was good that both of us were double majors and safe if we failed this class.

"First up, we've got Karolin and Luis. Get up here and start presenting," he barked, then sat down at his desk and crossed her arms over his chest.

Karolin and Luis walked to the front of the room and started running through their case study about a company that had found contamination in their baby formula. I started to feel a little bit better about this whole thing. Everyone had gotten equally difficult prompts about companies and people who had really screwed up, so Lilith and I weren't the only people who had to defend something totally terrible.

We had five minutes left in the class period when the last presentation wrapped up. Maybe this was going to be okay, because we would run out of time, and then we'd have to go to the next session.

But of course not. "We have three minutes left in class," Professor Jenkins announced. "And you might not think that that is long enough for a presentation, but in the real world, you don't get nicely scheduled sessions. This class prepares you for what's going to happen once the college stops coddling you. So Arielle and Lilith, get down here."

Lilith squeezed my hand, and I gave her as much of a smile as I could manage. At least I was going into this with a friend by my side. We reached the front of the room, and I cleared my throat.

"Are you going to start or not? Nobody wants to waste their time standing up here and looking at you," Professor Jenkins interrupted.

Lilith and I forced smiles. "We are responding to a fashion brand where the CEO made incendiary and fatphobic comments about people's weight," she started, then looked over at me.

I forced myself to smile. I was strong and smart and capable, and I could do this. "Our proposal is to counter the CEO's comments with something different. Rather than trying to respond to them by gaslighting the press, we want to make sure that we have a positive message. So we're going to announce the launch of a new, more inclusive line of athletic clothing for people – not just women – of all sizes, including for people who may need to use prosthetics or not be able to use zippers or buttons."

"Are you kidding me?" Professor Jenkins interrupted. His voice was so loud that I dropped my notecards. They went fluttering down onto the table. "The assignment was to come in and tell me how you were going to respond to the situation. Don't come in and give me some garbage about how the company needs to change!"

Lilith jumped in before I could. "Our thinking is that it's not possible for the company to respond well to the situation given its current market positioning. The company has non-inclusive branding and advertising, so the company is getting more and more backed into a corner. Given that such a large percentage of the US population is larger than a size four, we think the company needs to change to stay relevant."

"You girls are completely out of line," he snapped at us, standing up. "The assignment was to figure out how to respond to a negative company press event. Not to come in here and feed me some social justice warrior nonsense about how we have to change the entire company to make it different."

"That's not fair!" My voice cracked as I said it. He hadn't let us finish. We'd done the research. We'd found a line of inclusive clothing at Target that really helped its sales. We had statistics showing that people were willing to spend more money for clothes that reflected their values.

He didn't even stop. "With that, class is dismissed. We don't need to finish this one."

I stared at him. Nobody had moved from the classroom. "What you should have done," he continued, "is gone on the offensive. Doubled down on the comments. You either have to deny it and move on, or you can just say that it's true. Abercrombie used to say they only had cool, attractive models, because they weren't interested in having losers buy their clothes. And you know what happened? Fantastic sales."

"But it's not true," I said, swallowing. I wasn't even sure if I'd said it out loud. But everyone was still seated, listening. "I mean, that might be true with Abercrombie thirty years ago. But marketing is better now about being more inclusive, and you can't go back to having that kind of exclusionary brand image."

"We did the research!" Lilith said, taking a step towards me.

Professor Jenkins was standing up now, arms crossed over his chest. "Some research, you say? Should I remind you that I have decades of experience?"

The room was silent. No one had moved out of their seats.

If this was communications, if this was the real world, I didn't want it.

Professor Jenkins narrowed his eyes, staring at us. "You could have just gone on and pretended that it never happened. Denied it. It wasn't what he meant, you could have said every time that someone asked you about it. But you wanted to be all high and mighty about how you're right and moral and better than everyone else."

"It's not right to gaslight people," I managed. "I mean, if the CEO really believes that, shouldn't you think about replacing the CEO with someone who cares about the people you're selling clothes to?"

"You think that your job is to come in here and try to replace the CEO?" He actually snorted out loud. Like we were so dumb that all he could do was laugh. "Your job is to keep your head down. If you want to be in a class where you get to whine about how unfair the world is, go be an English major. You'll wake up when the only person who will hire you is Starbucks."

The classroom was still completely silent.

"Class is dismissed. Let's not waste any more of our time today." And with that, he stood up, walking out of the room. Our classmates followed him slowly, looking back over their shoulders at us as they left.

Lilith and I both stood there as the classroom emptied around us. "That was so bad," she said, reaching over to me and gripping my shoulder. Both of us were still trembling from the adrenaline.

"I can't believe that he was so unfair," I said. I took a deep breath, closing my eyes and trying to take slow breaths. "We spent so much time preparing for this."

"We have to do something about it," she said, looking at me. "There's being tough on your students, and there's berating them in front of the room."

"But what? You know the rumor that someone filed a complaint, but the school was too poor to fire him." We weren't the first people to have this happen. It sucked, but we knew it was a risk.

She looked at me. "I don't know. I think it might be good if we did it anyway. And we're both double majors, so we can afford to drop the class."

I hadn't thought of that. Lilith and I could graduate without our communications major, but the rest of our class couldn't. Maybe we could file a complaint, because what had happened had been obvious to everyone in class. "I don't know. You're right about the major, but I don't know. Do we just focus on moving on?"

She paused for a second, then shook her head. "I think we should file. I think it'll be good for closure, you know?"

I preferred forgetting to moving on. "I think you might be right. Can we talk more about it later?"

She nodded. "We definitely should. I have to get to class, but I'll text you." She reached over and gave me a hug. I squeezed her back. She turned towards the psychology building, and I headed the other way, looking for the café. I wasn't ready to go back to the apartment and have to think about what had happened, so I was going to go for a walk.

I could feel the tears starting to build in the corners of my eyes. Damn it. I wasn't going to cry in the middle of the hallway. I wasn't going to let Jenkins get to me this much. He had been an asshole, but I wasn't going to give him any more power over me.

I could deal with people being assholes. I was overreacting. I stopped and stared at the ceiling, blinking a couple times to force the tears back.

"Are you okay?"

Lucas appeared in front of me. He stuck his hands into his pockets, his backpack falling over one shoulder. "Are you crying?"

"No!" I was not going to cry. I wasn't going to be the sensitive snowflake Jenkins claimed I was.

"Can I get you anything? Hot chocolate, maybe?" he said, his eyes not leaving my face.

I swallowed. "I was going to get tea. You can come with me."

We reached the café in the middle of campus. Lucas ordered two giant mugs of hot chocolate and a muffin. I sat down at the table and stared at my hands. Jenkins was an asshole. That hadn't been fair. None of that had been fair.

"What happened?" he asked, coming back to the table and sliding a mug of hot chocolate towards me. Lucas knew what to do for bad days, which was always hot chocolate with extra whipped cream. Tea wasn't going to cut it here.

Part of me thought that he might be psychic. There were a few things that got me through bad times, and one of them was this exact drink. I'd gotten it plenty of times last year with Spencer, to the point where the people at the cafe had started making it as soon as I walked in.

"Professor Jenkins is an asshole," I said, cupping both of my hands around my hot chocolate and taking a drink.

"That's the professor for your senior seminar in communications?" Lucas asked, leaning forward. He pushed the muffin towards me. I tore off a chunk and stuffed it into my mouth.

I nodded. "He went off on us today. He called us social justice warriors, as though that's the worst thing that you could possibly be, and then he told us that we were shames to the major."

"In class? He actually said that to you in class?" Lucas's eyes had gotten wide, and he leaned forward towards me. "You have to file a complaint or something, Arielle. That's so out of line."

I wasn't ready for solutions right now. I just wanted to be angry and eat my muffin. "Yeah, I know."

"If he's really so bad that he's making you cry, that's not normal," Lucas replied, not quite getting the message. "I mean, there's being a tough professor, but that's totally different than making you cry in front of everyone."

Lucas clearly still lived in a world where things were fair. "Maybe he's right. Maybe I'm just too soft for the real world. I'm going to get a real job, and I'm going to get eaten alive. If I even get a job with my English major."

"No one at actual jobs can do that either. You have whole HR teams for that. That can't be normal work behavior, and so there's no reason that school should tolerate it either."

My mom and dad definitely acted just like Professor Jenkins. Lucas could say the world was a better place than that, but he hadn't hung out with my parents.

Spencer stopped at the table. I looked up at her, blinking a few times so that she couldn't see the frustrated tears in my eyes. "Arielle?" she asked.

"Jenkins was an asshole," Lucas said, filling Spence in on the entire situation in four words. Spencer reached over and wrapped me in a hug.

The campus bells started ringing, and Lucas stood up. "I'm sorry, Arielle. I have to go to class. Talk later, okay?"

As though there was more than I wanted to talk about in this situation. The only thing that I wanted to do was be angry. Clearly, my best friend wasn't reading that on my face.

As soon as Lucas walked away, Spencer pulled out

a chair and sat down directly in front of me. "Okay. We are going to talk about this."

"Do I have my I want to talk about this face on right now?" I reached for the muffin and tore another chunk off.

"Earlier this year, you told me Jenkins called someone a dumb woman in front of the whole class because they weren't able to answer a question quickly enough. Even after he randomly called on her and didn't give her any time to think," Spencer replied. She leaned in towards the table and grabbed a piece of muffin. "He's the worst. I don't understand why you keep going back to that class."

"I have to." I didn't quite understand why they weren't getting this part of the conversation. "I'm a communications major. This is the required senior seminar for communications. I have to take it."

"You know that there is a solution to that, right?" she said.

I looked at her, reaching for the muffin. "I thought you were the one who was telling me to stick it out to graduate with the major. One class left and all that."

"Yeah, but when your professor makes you cry in front of the whole class, I change my mind." She put her forearms on the table, leaning closer towards me. "Ari. You deserve more than that."

"I do!" I wasn't going to argue about that. It was a bad situation. "But you know that my parents are only funding communications?"

"Right." Spencer didn't know quite everything about how I was paying for college, but she did know that my parents had flipped out about my English major. They'd told me that if I wanted to throw away my life, they'd support it when I was also taking communications.

When I'd broken up with Nate, they'd yanked the money they were paying for English credits. I could usually cover the rest with my ghostwriting income, but right now my job was on the line.

"I'm so close to graduating, so why would I throw that away and just make it tougher for myself?" I didn't want to admit it, but what if Nate had been right all along? Margaret Siskind thought my writing was terrible and our line was in trouble. Maybe that wasn't going to be an option much longer.

"I get that. But the class is making you cry. That's not okay," she said.

There were many things in my life that could make me cry. This class wasn't even the least of it. I'd take getting called a social justice warrior over getting fired from ghostwriting any day. "Spence. It's going to be okay."

She stared at me for a second, her eyes narrowing. She knew that I was lying. She knew that it wasn't okay, and that I was just saying it to get myself to believe. But there must have been something on my face that convinced her to stop asking. "Okay. At least drink your hot chocolate."

Chapter 12

I woke up two days later to a text from my parents. *Have you booked your flight home for your father's birthday yet?*

Damn it. I had forgotten that I had to go home for that this year. It was going to be a blowout party. Five years ago, my parents had rented an entire beachfront club, complete with an out of work troupe of belly dancers and a suckling pig. The entire thing had been ripped off reality television.

And I knew which other family was going to be there. Their business partners and parents of the worst people in the world. Nate Kingston and his whole family.

I started to type something back, then stopped. *I can't make it,* I wanted to send.

Maybe Nate wouldn't be there this year. He was too busy sleeping with anyone who would sleep with him.

And anyway, it was only a weekend. I could make it through a weekend.

I stared down at my phone for another second, then shut the screen and stuffed it into my pocket. I'd make myself a deal. I could go drop my major, or I could answer that text.

With two sucky choices, it was a whole lot easier. I pulled on a jacket and headed out towards the administrative buildings. I had only been in it a couple of times to drop off forms before.

I stopped in the lobby, checking the signs towards the registrar's office. I could totally do this. I could walk in there, drop communications, and deal with the fallout from my parents later.

I took a deep breath and pushed open the door. "Do you have an appointment?" the receptionist asked as I walked in.

I shook my head. "Nope."

"So I assume you're okay talking to whoever is first available," she said, glancing down at her computer screen. "And you're in luck. Third door on the right. Room seven. It's one of our associate deans."

I nodded and smiled, heading past the desk and down through a hallway. It was the same generic corporate hallway as the rest of the building, which was strangely comforting. This was just like going to renew my driver's license.

I turned into room seven, where the associate

dean was sitting behind a desk. "Welcome! Sit down and close the door, if you wouldn't mind."

Closing the door was only going to make me more nervous. "And what can I help you with?" she asked as I took a seat. The chairs were sized for children.

"I wanted to see about dropping my major," I said. I was saying the words out loud. "I'm a senior, and I'm doing a communications major right now. But I want to drop it. And I want to drop Professor Jenkins's class."

She stared at me for a second, and then nodded. She tapped on her computer and started to pull up what must have been my transcript. "So if you drop that class, it means that you'll only be registered in three classes this semester."

I nodded. "But I should have extra credits from when I did AP classes in high school. And a couple of my English classes have extra credit hours because they had workshops, too. So I think that I should be okay with graduating."

"And you're also an English major, so you wouldn't have any issue with the major requirement," she said, continuing to scroll through my transcript. She tapped a few keys, then looked up at me. "Looking at your profile, what I'd actually recommend is staying in the class. We can remove it from your transcript later if it's an issue, but unless you're going to fail the course, it would still give you a shot to get the major."

I blinked, a tear suddenly forming in my eye. "I think that I'm going to fail the class, so that's not relevant."

"Why are you sure?" she asked, turning her chair towards me and leaning forward. "We still have plenty of time in the semester to turn things around, and plenty of resources if you're struggling."

"Professor Jenkins told me that I was a social justice warrior," I said. Deep breath. "Actually, if it's okay, I think I might want to file a complaint. I was thinking about it, and even if I drop the class, I want to make sure there's a record of it."

She nodded. "If your professor is creating an environment where you feel like you can't be in class, then you should definitely file something. I can't promise what the outcome will be, but I can tell you that we take all complaints seriously."

"And I'm not scared of tough professors," I added. I'd had Professor Shriver my sophomore year, and she was the toughest person I'd ever met. She didn't take excuses, and she made me rewrite one paper four times. But she did it because she wanted to make me better, and I was a much better writer after that class.

"Being tough and being mean are two different things," the dean said, leaning towards me. "And that's why we have an investigation process. "Why don't I send you the materials over email, and you can make an appointment and decide if you want to move forward?"

I nodded. "I can do that." I wanted to talk to Lilith first anyway. The complaint had been her idea, and she would probably join me in it.

"So going back to your class," she said, tapping a few buttons. "I'm going to leave you enrolled in the class for now and add a note in your file that you can drop it later. And you said you also wanted to drop your major?"

I swallowed. It was stupid to drop the major at this point, when there was a chance that i could pass senior seminar anyway. But communications was part of my past now, and I didn't want to keep the major. "Yeah. I'd like to drop it."

She tapped a few buttons on her computer. "And, done."

"Wait, that was it?" I asked, leaning forward.

Part of me had expected that there was going to be more drama. More forms, a giant signing ceremony, something. *Arielle is pissing off her parents and deciding to do something she loves, even though they don't understand why.*

She turned towards me and nodded. "We're here to help you make the most of college. You're saying you don't want to be a communications major. You've had three and a half years in that major to think about it, so I'm going to trust that you know what you're doing."

"Thank you," I said again, standing up. "I didn't think it was going to be that easy."

"You should have come and seen us sooner," she said, nodding towards her computer screen. "I don't want to have students stuck in programs they hate. Come back if you need any advice on anything. But it seems like you've got everything under control."

"Thanks," I said, standing up and walking out of her office, closing the door behind me. I waved to the receptionist as I walked out of the office and down the hallway back towards the elevator. I had actually done it. I had dropped communications. The thing that I had only done because Nate and my parents had told me that I had to do it.

And now I was going to prove them wrong. I was going to show them I'd have a career even if I wasn't a communications major. I wasn't going to let what they thought, and what stupid Professor Jenkins thought, control my life. I was going to do it myself.

I was doing this for me. Not for them, not for anyone else. I wasn't even doing it for my friends. Just for me.

I paused on the street as I left the administrative building. It seemed like an excellent time to go celebrate. I turned and headed off in the direction of the best baked goods in town.

"AND SO YOU just dropped the major?"

When I told the story about how I had dropped my communications major to Raleigh and Spencer, I might have made it sound slightly more dramatic than it had actually been in real life. Having the associate dean click a few buttons wasn't quite the story I had been going for.

"Good job. Why would you waste your time taking a major that you weren't interested in?" Spencer asked, leaning forward and clapping me on the shoulder. "I wouldn't want to have to spend hours in class worrying about things that I didn't care about. Or that I wasn't going to use in my normal life."

"And you're going to use quantum physics in daily life?" Raleigh asked, reaching forward and grabbing a cinnamon roll bite. It really was the best thing to have friends who stress baked.

"Knowing about math is important," Spencer replied. "There are so many billions of applications of math to daily life, not just calculating restaurant tips."

"Are we forgetting that we are supposed to be celebrating the fact that I never thought that I was going to be brave enough to drop the communications major, and I did it?" I asked, looking in between the two of them. "Don't you dare get into an argument about quantum physics right now."

"It's not an argument. It's a spirited discussion. Two very different things," Spencer replied.

"I hate it when the two of you argue. It's like

seeing your parents argue or something," I mumbled. I reached for another cinnamon roll bite, popping it into my mouth. "So what are we going to watch?"

"Can we watch something that isn't dark?" Raleigh asked, sticking her feet up on the coffee table. "I want a romantic comedy with a dumb plot that I can laugh at."

"There's nothing wrong with movies that make you think," Spencer objected.

"The last thing that you made us watch was, like, a legit spy thriller about people trying to prevent a nuclear bomb explosion. It was not light and fluffy. I want light and fluffy. And it's my apartment."

It was Raleigh's apartment, but in fairness, she refused to come to ours because Lilyanna had separation anxiety. But since Raleigh was the one who made all of the baked goods, and Lilyanna was very cute, we didn't complain too much. "But," Spencer said, turning towards me, "Arielle is the one who dropped her major, and that means that we're celebrating her. So she gets to pick the movie."

"You're really putting me on the spot here." I didn't really have a genre of movies that I liked so much as that I liked good movies. And that meant movies where I wasn't rolling my eyes halfway through at poorly developed characters.

People made fun of romance novels for having poor character development and being too predictable, but had they seen most action movies? Or most rom coms? They were all terrible. It was like the male characters always had a dead girlfriend, which was supposed to explain why they were being assholes to everyone around them. And we were supposed to let them get away with it.

Ugh. I had so many feelings. How did people who were so bad at writing women get so much screentime?

"Can't we just watch something on TV? It's less decision fatigue, and it's less time that we have to commit to watching it if you guys don't agree on what we're watching." There had been a few times where it had been apparent ten minutes into a movie that we were going to hear Raleigh and Spencer bicker, and I was stuck listening for the rest of the two hours.

"Great idea," Raleigh said, grabbing the remote from in front of me and starting to scroll through the options. "What about – "

"No," Spencer said without even looking up from her phone. "I know what you are scrolling to, and I do not approve."

"But – " Raleigh started.

"Don't even think about it. You are going to think that it is swoonworthy, and I am going to think that it looks like the worst sex that I have ever seen on TV. We are not going to agree on what we are going to watch," Spencer replied.

"Are we just going to end up watching the Great British Baking Show again?" I asked. It was one of our few compromise shows that seemed to be acceptable to everyone, and that meant that we had watched all of it. Twice.

"Great idea," Raleight said, scrolling through Netflix a little longer. "Excellent pastry, here we come."

"If you promise to make more of these for me, I won't complain about your TV selection." Spencer grabbed another one of the miniature cinnamon buns and settled down onto the couch.

Before we made it through the opening credits, the door swung open. "I love this show," came a very familiar voice from the doorway.

I turned to see Lucas and Mason walking in with Luisa and Tyler. "This is so much better than what I was hoping for when I came over," Luisa said, walking towards the couch and waving towards us. "Hey there."

"It's bread week, and you know what that means," Spencer said, turning towards us. There was a giant smear of cinnamon sugar on the side of her mouth. "This is one of the most intense weeks of the entire season."

"How much of this have you watched?" Tyler asked, coming up behind the couch. He'd come over to a few of the movie nights, but usually had language lab late at night, so had missed a lot of our weekday watch parties.

"All of it," Raleigh replied. "There is very little

TV that we agree on, and this is about it. So this is what we are going to watch every time."

"You can't agree on what TV to watch, so you watch a bunch of British people make bread?" Tyler asked.

Raleigh turned towards them, then reached down and handed them part of her cinnamon bun. "You don't understand. This show is basically therapy for my soul. It's aggressively wholesome."

"Scoot over." There was pressure on my leg, and I looked up to see Lucas standing there. My heart rate immediately jumped up about five thousand beats per minute. Spencer might have told me that that was mathematically improbable, but it felt like it.

I scooted into Raleigh's side. She moved slightly over, but Luisa had taken her other side. "Oh, I love bread week," Luisa said. She'd been skeptical a show about amateurs baking could be exciting, but we'd managed to indoctrinate her into the cult.

"So how are things going?" Lucas asked. His fingers drummed on his leg next to mine. "I heard you dropped the major."

"How did you hear that?" I turned towards him.

"Mason told me," he said. He leaned forward and grabbed one of the last cinnamon rolls off of the central table. His shirt rode up slightly as he did, and I forced myself to look away. I wasn't going to stare at him. That was inappropriate.

"I clearly wasn't going to pass the major if I failed

my senior seminar, and anyway, I didn't want to finish it," I said. I wasn't going to do it just because my parents said that I should.

"You didn't want to finish it despite having done it all this time?" His eyes were on my face.

Oh man, I really didn't want to have to talk about this topic. Because I didn't want to talk about Nate, basically ever, but I especially didn't want to have to talk about Nate with Lucas. Who was sitting right here and leaning into me. "No. And anyway, we're celebrating. Because I did the thing that I wanted to do and dropped the major."

He stared at me for a second, as though he wanted to keep asking questions. Then he nodded and leaned back on the couch. "Okay. As long as you're happy about it, I'm happy about it."

That was exactly what I needed to hear. I was happy, and I had done this for myself, and it didn't matter if I could explain it or not.

My phone buzzed with a text from Lilith. *Proud of you. My appointment is tomorrow morning to get the complaint paperwork!*

"I'm filing a complaint with the school about Professor Jenkins," I said quietly, looking at Lucas.

"Really?" His eyebrows shot up. "You finally decided to do it?"

I took a deep breath. "Yeah. Lilith and I are both going to do it. We decided that it wasn't fair, what he said to us, and that we were going to at least say something."

"I'm proud of you," he said, his hand drifting towards my leg.

I smiled. I was proud of me, too, and that was the important thing. "Thanks, Lucas."

I turned my attention back towards the TV, where the normal cast of characters were aggressively kneading bread dough. There was something so relaxing about watching a group of people making bread because they wanted to. Not because there was some kind of big prize, or this would save their business or something, but because they liked being and bragging rights. It was nice. Wholesome.

Lucas's phone rang, and he pulled it out of his pocket. He stared down at it for a few seconds, then stood up. "Be right back."

"Okay," I said, glancing towards him. My voice wavered as I said it, like there was part of me that was wondering why he felt like he needed to excuse himself from sitting next to me.

I kept watching as a bunch of British people kneaded their bread, but there was a voice in the back of my head that wouldn't shut up. *What is Lucas doing back there on his phone? Is it another girl? Is that why he didn't want to take the call in front of you?*

Not that that was any of my business. Lucas and I weren't together. Lucas and I were friends, and maybe

I wanted us to be something more, but I wasn't even totally sure about that.

I forced myself to pay attention to the show again. In true form, Spencer was the toughest critic. "Of course you have to put cold water in. It's basic science," she said, shaking her head at the screen. "You should get sent home today."

Raleigh looked over. "That's not nice, Spence! There are so many things to remember, and you have to remember that no one on this show is a professional."

"By now, you should be a professional," she said, pointing at the screen. "Do you know how many seasons of this show there are? You should know what's coming. You have to do your research before you're in front of the entire world."

"Just appreciate what they can do, Spencer," Luisa said, apparently deciding to take pity on Raleigh.

We reached the first round of judging, and I glanced around at everyone else on the couch. I was going to have to go to the bathroom, and I didn't want them to pause the show so that I could see judging. That had happened once, and Spence and Raleigh had counted how long it had taken me to pee before they could resume watching.

I wasn't in the mood to have my bladder timed today, so I was going to have to go before there was a big moment in the show. "I'm going to the bathroom. Don't pause it," I said, getting up and extracting myself from the couch. Raleigh had done of those overly squishy couches that made it almost impossible to get up and out of it. Great for napping, not great for studying.

I hopped over the tangle of legs out in front of the couch and walked towards the bathroom. I opened the door and locked it behind me, then stared at the lock for a second. I was totally going to be able to undo this one. Not that I had been having nightmares about getting locked in bathrooms recently or anything.

But I was a big fan of bathrooms with windows now. I'd never appreciated how useful windows were for getting out of sticky situations.

I went to the bathroom, then washed my hands and walked out of the bathroom, directly into Lucas. He was on the phone, pacing in the second bedroom. "Seriously, Dad, I'm fine." There was another pause. "I know. I know you're worried. But I am totally fine. I can manage."

I stopped in the doorway, looking at him. His eyes met mine. "Yeah, I'm at Raleigh's," he said, rolling his eyes at me. "And yes, we're watching the show with the bread. Raleigh and Spencer are getting heated."

I snorted, and on the other end, I could hear his mom's voice. "Raleigh and Spencer are there? Is Mason? Can we say hi?"

I would say hi to Lucas's parents any day. "Hi!" I

said, loudly enough that I hoped that they could hear me on the other end.

"Who's that?" his dad's voice asked.

I stepped into the room. Lucas put the phone on speaker, holding it out in front of me. "Hi, it's Arielle," I said.

"Arielle!" His mom sounded genuinely thrilled to hear my voice. "Are you reading any good books that you can recommend? I just finished my book for book club this month, and I need something new."

Lucas looked like he wanted to roll his eyes again, but I didn't let him. "Mom, we do have to get back to watching the bread making. Raleigh and Spencer will pause judging for us if we don't get back there."

"They have before," I added. "They used to time my bathroom breaks."

"That is dedication," Lucas's dad said, sounding impressed despite himself.

"Well, we won't keep you then! Have a great weekend, you two!"

"Bye," his dad called, and they hung up the phone.

Lucas sighed, running a hand through his hair and sticking his phone back into his pocket. "We got off easy that time. Last time, my parents asked me what bread they were making, and then my mom shipped me a loaf of it at school."

"Your parents are so cool." I would take parents

who shipped me bread any day. That sounded like the absolute best kind of parent.

"My parents are experts at being embarrassing," he said, leaning down towards me, very close.

I swallowed, looking up at him, my stomach flipping. But before anything else could happen, Raleigh turned her head towards the two of us. "Get back here! It's judging."

"And bring more snacks!" Spencer called, not moving her head away from the television.

Lucas looked down at me, half of his mouth twisting up into a smile. "I think we have orders."

Chapter 13

"Okay, I promised not to suggest baking for the party, but I really think this whole atmosphere could be improved with some baked goods," Raleigh said, standing in the middle of the room with her hands on her hips.

Spencer had passed a midterm in quantum physics that was supposed to be notoriously difficult, and Raleigh had firmly suggested that we should throw a party to celebrate. So now we were throwing a party.

"I really don't think that people are going to come to this party because they want baked goods," I said, looking up and around the apartment. I set my laptop to the side, willing myself not to look at the calendar invitation.

"False. Everyone loves baked goods." She shook

her head again. "There's just something missing here."

"It wouldn't be alcohol and drunk people, would it?" Spencer had promised to go out and pick up alcohol later, as long as we had enough duct tape to repair Lazzie.

It was a good thing that Spencer's many years of science education had taught her how to fix anything with duct tape. One of the rear door handles had fallen off last week, and Spencer had stuck it right back on.

"Yes, but those are coming." She stared at the room again, tilting her head to the side. "You know what it is? Fairy lights. You don't have fairy lights."

"We have literally never had fairy lights before at a party, and we've had plenty of good parties," I replied, looking up from my computer, where I was pretending to read an article for communications.

"I don't know why, but they're speaking to me right now. And they're telling me that they're missing." She turned towards me, putting her hands on her hips. "I'm going to Target."

Sending Raleigh to Target by herself was dangerous. She wasn't going to come back for a couple hours, and when she did, there was going to be more stuff with her than we possibly knew what to do with. Raleigh loved decorating things, especially things that didn't belong to her, like my apartment.

Last year, she'd gotten excited about a sale on rubber ducks and bought us several dozen rubber ducks. Spencer had built a robot to launch them around the room. I was still finding them in my dresser.

"You are not seriously going to go to Target and insist on buying fairy lights for this party right now," I replied. "Remember the duck debacle."

I should have known better than to try to argue with Raleigh. "Those were on sale! And they really did brighten up the apartment. You need decorations to give the place character."

"Right." I still wasn't convinced, but I wasn't going to waste any more time arguing. Raleigh was more like Spencer than she admitted. When one of them got an idea, it was happening, no matter what.

She grinned. "Okay. I'm picking some things up. Don't even think about telling me that this is a bad idea."

"Trust me, I can't tell you anything is a bad idea," I called after her as she grabbed her wallet and headed down the stairs.

I sat down on the couch and pulled my laptop back onto my lap. There wasn't much party prep that I could do until Spencer arrived with the alcohol.

My phone rang, and I picked it up without looking at the caller ID. "Hello?"

"This is Margaret Siskind. Your editor?"

I had totally forgotten that I was supposed to talk to her today about my chapters. I knew that I had something to do today. "I was just waiting for your call," I said, in the least convincing excuse that I could have come up with.

"Great. I'm calling about the chapters that you sent in," she said, her voice flat.

My heart started pounding. "I did. I mean, I sent in chapters," I added quickly.

They hadn't been the best chapters, but done was better than perfect, or something like that. Plus, that was part of writing. Sometimes you had to write some terrible first drafts and send them over.

"I'm going to just say this straight out. These are not good chapters" she said.

My heart felt like it had stopped. No one had told me that before. I mean, maybe they weren't the best pages that I had ever written, but they also weren't the worst. "I don't think they're that bad," I finally managed. "It meets all the requirements for the genre."

Margaret sighed on the other end. "That is technically true, but you haven't made me care about any of the characters in this to read it. Trust me, you can't write a sex scene hot enough to make that worth it."

She thought that my writing was flat? Lifeless? I stared at the cabinets, my brain still trying to process the words. Emma had only ever said nice things.

Margaret took another deep breath on the other end. "Look, Arielle. I know this is hard to hear. I'm going to give you some unsolicited advice here. Get out of your own head for a while, stop worrying about genre rules, and try to write a love story."

This couldn't actually be happening to me. Writing was the only thing that I was good at. I had just dropped communications, and writing was all that was left. I couldn't be bad at it. I couldn't fail like this, not when it was supposed to be my job after I graduated.

"I didn't think that it was that bad." I should stop defending myself, said the voice in the back of my head. Just admit that it was bad and move on. Promise to fix it all in edits, even if I didn't have a clue how I was going to do that. I could fix it. I could find a way.

"Let's talk about examples then." Keys clacked in the background of the call. "You build Lord Bennington up to have some terrible family secret."

"But isn't having a secret twin brother a family secret?" Yeah, it hadn't been my best idea but in my defense, it was more believable than the plot twists on many of the things Raleigh watched.

I heard a snort on the other end. "Sure, but it doesn't excuse him being a boring asshole for the rest of the book. Lady Beverly is supposed to like the man, and ignoring the obvious lack of chemistry or shared interests between them, she flits around complaining about the fact that he is paying attention to her and that he likes her. She likes him. You just want to scream at her to woman up and tell him."

All of this was technically true. It wasn't good, but that didn't mean that I wanted to hear it. It was a good thing we weren't on video. "But it's romance," I said, my voice weak.

"The reason that people say terrible things about romance as a genre is that we've let shallow plots and sex writing stand in for character development," she shot back.

"I can turn in edits." That was the only thing that I could think of. Because if she was this mad about what I had written, it wasn't going to be good for me. I was going to have to figure out what I was going to do to save my job.

She took a deep breath. "Yes. I need edits. To be honest, I'm pretty disappointed in what you turned in."

Disappointment was the absolute worst. It was worse than if she'd just been mad at me, because I could have dealt with that a whole lot better. "I'll do better," I said, my voice small.

"Let's talk about what you've done well in the past so that you can learn from that," she replied. I heard her keys clacking in the background again. "Your only thing rated four stars was *His Lady of the Manor.*"

Oh god. I closed my eyes for a second.

His Lady novels were the worst things that I had ever written. I was embarrassed that I had even strung a lot of the sentences together that made up those books. They were about women who had managed to seduce perfect husbands, and then they found happiness when they gave up all their dreams and just became supporting characters.

They were terrible. I had written them when I was still with Nate. I had written in everything that I wanted to feel for Nate. I papered over all our problems with my book. Because I had my wonderful boyfriend, and we had our family businesses, and we were going to settle down to the life that our parents had created for us. If my characters did it, I could too.

The comments hadn't been great. It had been a lot of people pointing out that the book seemed totally anti-feminist, but then a few people pointing out that feminism meant equality, not that women couldn't choose supporting roles in the relationship. Then a church group in the south recommended it as a guide for fundamental religious relationships. They'd highlighted it as a romance with conservative, traditional ideas.

And that had driven my sales way up. It should have probably told me that I was on the wrong track with writing them, but my brain was so addled from Nate that I totally missed that.

"That book was thematically problematic," I said, in what was the nicest thing I could say about my own writing.

"Agree," she said, her keyboard still clacking. "A terrible model of what a healthy relationship should be. But at least it had feelings in it. That's the difference between it and what you just sent me."

I was never going back to writing those. I couldn't write the novels that were about my happy ending with Nate. "I'll fix what I wrote. I'll get you edits." I had to keep this job.

"That's what I wanted to hear. Get me those edits, and email if you want to talk more. I know it's tough feedback, but I believe in you and will support you through the revisions."

"Thanks," I said, swallowing. With that, Margaret Siskind hung up the phone.

I dropped my phone and stared at the opposite wall. Writing had always gotten me through. I had been flying home to see my parents, and I had stopped in an airport bookstore. And I had gone straight for the romance novels, and I had stared at one of the things I had written. Actually on the shelf, there, in print.

And it sounded totally stupid to say now, but that was what had kept me going. Knowing that I had written something that was out there in the world.

Losing Nate didn't make me a failure. Not at all. I was going to be strong and independent without him. Those romance novels, as much fun as people made of them, had helped me do that.

But once I had given up writing the terrible ones that were about Nate, I hadn't found anything to replace them. I hadn't figured out how to write a novel about healthy relationships yet, only about Nate. I hadn't written my new dreams, only my old ones.

I walked around the apartment, staring at the ceiling. God. I knew that I hadn't written something great, but it was when you turned in a paper knowing it wasn't your best, and you ended up failing, not just getting a B. Maybe it wasn't an A manuscript, but it should have been better than this.

Maybe you shouldn't have dropped communications, said that same voice in the back of my head. *Maybe you should have thought about whether you were actually good enough to become a full time writer before you went ahead and tried to do it, hmm?*

I really hated that voice.

The door pushed open, and Raleigh walked into the apartment, a dozen reusable Target bags hanging from her arms. She looked at me and then stopped dead in her tracks. "Ari? Are you okay?"

I had to get out of my own head. I was having people over, and I was supposed to be getting ready for a party. If I was going to write the book that I needed to write, I had to get over Nate for good. I had to put that behind me and write the new ending. Even if I couldn't figure out how to do that right now.

"Of course," I said, blinking a few times and turning towards her. "Just thinking about some stuff for class. What do you want me to do?"

Chapter 14

Raleigh had been right about the fairy lights.

It was three hours later, and the apartment was already starting to fill up. Raleigh had hung the fairy lights all over the apartment and covered them in chiffon, which if anyone else had done it, would have made this look like a bad high school dance. But when Raleigh did it, it made it look like we were at a high end club.

I refilled my wine glass and started to wander towards the kitchen. Spencer had turned up the music as loud as we could make it on our terrible speakers, and it occasionally got too scratchy to hear.

I took a sip of my wine and stared around the room again. "Great party," Luisa said, coming up beside me.

"I didn't know that you were going to be able to make it!" Luisa had told me earlier in the week that she was thinking about studying instead of coming out. "Did Raleigh guilt trip you?"

She snorted. "Not Raleigh. This one was all Mason. He told me that he'd take the next patient who was inventing an illness if I came."

"That's something." Both Luisa and Mason were in the pre-med program, Luisa studying to be a psychologist and Mason a dentist. "I didn't know that Mason was that excited about us having a party."

"Oh, he told me that he thought that it was going to be the worst, and it was going to be totally annoying, and that there was no way he was missing it," she replied, reaching into the fridge. "Mind if I grab some wine?"

"Oh no, go for it," I said, nodding towards the fridge. I reached in and pulled out one of the bottles, passing it over to her. "I'd be a terrible host if I didn't give you anything to drink."

She laughed slightly, tossing some of her hair back. She was one of those people who made any movement look elegant and put together, no matter how small. "I still plan on studying tonight, so I'm going to limit myself to one. But thanks."

Of course Luisa was going to be the responsible one. "You came out to a party and are having a single glass of wine? When did you get so classy?"

She grinned at me. "To be honest, I was really just hoping that there were going to be baked goods. That was the real reason that I came out." She reached over and clinked her glass against mine. "How are you feeling being a single major now?"

Of all the questions to ask me right now. I had dropped the practical communications major, and now I only had the major in English. And my editor was about to fire me, and I'd never been able to write something that wasn't about Nate. "So awesome," I said, forcing my voice to be light. I could totally fool Luisa.

"Are you nervous about job stuff?" she asked. Thank god, she'd misinterpreted my voice.

"It's just weird because I've been a major for so long," I lied.

"I totally see that. It's brave of you to drop it this late, you know?" She took a sip of her wine. "I admire that about you. You figured something out about yourself and you went for it."

I wasn't brave. Not right now. I was the world's biggest fraud. I couldn't write a book that wasn't about Nate, and I couldn't finish my major.

Time to change the topic before I ruined the mood. "Yeah. There are a lot of people here, aren't there?"

"It's Raleigh," Luisa replied. Raleigh's baked goods were basically famous, to the point where her department had seen an uptick in people coming to tutoring sessions after Raleigh started bringing the snacks. "Do you mind if I head off and find some?"

"Of course not," I said. Luisa clinked her wine

glass against mine and then headed off into the party to try to find baked goods. I leaned against the counter and looked out at the party. I was feeling better, or at least I could tell myself that I was feeling better.

"Hey." I turned to see Lucas coming up beside me. He was dressed up slightly, wearing a nice t-shirt over khakis. He was attractive, and a big part of me knew it. "Are you just hanging back here and watching other people drinking?"

My heart started pounding. I started to feel dizzy and tried to take a deep breath. I was going to be okay. I wasn't going to let this happen. "I'm hosting. I'm hosting the party."

He grinned and leaned against the counter. He stretched his legs out in front of him, long enough that they took up the space from the counter back to the cabinets. "And your definition of hosting is standing over here and watching other people. Got it."

"I was going to go talk to people, but then someone came up and started talking to me." I forced myself to try to focus. My headache was getting worse, starting to feel dizzy again.

He nodded towards me. "Right. I'm glad you're talking to me with your very busy hosting."

I turned towards him. The side of his mouth had completely turned up into a smile now. "You are making fun of me."

"No idea why you would think that," he replied, taking a step towards me.

I swallowed. Focus, brain, focus. It felt like a panic attack coming on. I couldn't let that happen, not in the middle of the party. "Raleigh bought the fairy lights," I blurted out.

"The fairy lights?" he asked. He'd taken another step closer towards me. He was so much taller than I was, my head barely reaching his shoulder.

"She went to Target. We're all lucky to be alive." I could do this. I could pull myself back. I took a deep breath, then another one.

"But she did make it look quite romantic, don't you think?" he asked, his voice low. He was looking down at me, and I tilted my head back slightly.

Like I was going to kiss him.

There was a crash from the other side of the room. I instinctively took a step back, away from Lucas and all my thoughts, hitting one of the wine bottles. "Can you bring paper towels?" someone called to me.

Raleigh had knocked over a vase of flowers, which had spilled across the floor. She was laughing, her arms wrapped around Mason, her head thrown back.

I'd written a scene like this. It was the climax scene in His Lady of the Manor. It was candles, not fairy lights, but it was the same scene.

I couldn't keep looking at the two of them. It was bringing back too much, Nate and the novels I'd written about Nate and how maybe I could never be that happy again. "Paper towels," I said, the words turning into a mantra. "Paper towels, paper towels, paper towels."

"Ari?" Lucas's voice came from above me.

Before I could turn and look at him, I grabbed the paper towels and strode into the center of the room. "I've got them."

I reached Raleigh. She turned towards me. She slid her arms out from around Mason's neck and glanced back towards me. "Thanks, babe."

He reached down and pulled her back towards him. "I've got it."

The voices in the back of my head kept getting louder and louder, the dizziness more intense.

The only good thing that you ever wrote was about how you wanted a happily ever after with Nate. And then he left you. And you've never written anything good since.

You're a failure, Arielle. No one loves you, and you can't even write about it.

Raleigh turned back towards Mason. He picked up one of the flowers from the floor and stuck it in her hair, reaching forward and giving her a kiss.

I couldn't breathe. I had to get out of here.

I turned towards the door and sprinted out of the apartment. I needed the silence. I needed to be away from everything, to be alone I couldn't be at the party any more.

I ran up the stairs and out the fire door, onto the

roof. I sat down immediately, closing my eyes against the dizziness.

It's just a panic attack. You're going to be okay.

I wrapped my arms around my knees. I dropped my head down, resting it on my knees. *Breathe, Arielle. Just breathe.*

Chapter 15

The cold air was good for me. The waves of panic were starting to recede a little bit, and I took another deep breath.

This is a panic attack. You had them with the Nate stuff. You're getting through it.

I sat in the quiet for a few more moments, closing my eyes against the world. Without the noise of the party, I could feel my breathing start to regulate, my thoughts slow down.

"Arielle?"

I whipped my head around to see Lucas's silhouette in the doorway. "Hey," I said, the word coming out as a whisper.

"Hey," he said, taking a couple steps towards me, leaving distance between us. "I came to apologize."

I stared at him for a second. My breathing was slower, the waves receding. "Apologize?" I asked.

He nodded and walked closer towards me. "I mean, I saw that you got really panicked and left the party. And I wanted to apologize for being too pushy." He took a step towards me, then paused, his eyes roaming over my face. "Can I sit down?"

I nodded. He folded his legs and sat down next to me, two feet between us. Far enough away that he wasn't in my space, close enough that I could still see him. "I realized I've been pretty pushy., and that's not fair to you. I know that it's your choice whether you like me or not. If you want me to go away, just tell me."

I stared at him for another second. He was giving me options. He was listening to me, and he was asking me what I wanted. He was letting me make the choice.

But I still didn't know if I was strong enough to make a choice. Not when thinking about Nate still gave me a panic attack.

It's okay, Arielle. You made it. It was just a panic attack.

"You don't have to tell me," he said quickly, running a hand through his hair. "I get it. I don't want to ever make you feel like you have to run away from me. I don't know how I can just be friends with you, but I'm not entitled to have you like me just because you're my friend. I'm not that kind of asshole who would think that and – yeah. I'm sorry for being so pushy earlier."

I swallowed and looked away, staring out at the

street. *No, no, that's not it,* I wanted to say, but I couldn't get the words out.

"Do you want me to leave?" he asked, his voice dropping lower.

This was it. This was the time where I had to find my voice. "No," I said, my voice quiet. I turned towards him, swallowing again. "It wasn't you. I had a panic attack."

"That wasn't me, was it?" he said, his eyes sad. His hand started to reach towards me and then pulled back.

Maybe it was the fact that it was nighttime, and we were on the roof, just the two of us. I could say what I felt out loud, because this wouldn't feel real tomorrow.

"No," I said. And that was enough to get my words starting again, to get everything that I'd been keeping bottled up flowing.

"I like you, Lucas." The words sounded stronger than I expected, and it was like I knew how right they were as soon as I said them. "I guess I'm still trying to process some stuff that happened."

"Do you want to talk about it?" He hadn't moved closer, still giving me the space that I needed.

It's time, the back of my brain said. *You can do this. You can talk about it.*

"I do," I said. The answer seemed to reverberate around the street, and part of me expected something dramatic to happen, the world to stop spinning, the streets to explode, something. But of course, in life, nothing was ever that dramatic. I didn't need a swell of background music to let me know this moment mattered.

"Things ended with me and Nate not that long ago. I mean, you know that," I said, still looking at the street. I couldn't see Lucas's face as I told him the whole story. I didn't want sympathy from someone I wanted to be attractive to. "And what I told everyone was that it was a mutual thing. But that wasn't even close to the truth."

"Shit," I heard Lucas mutter, his voice tense. I didn't turn to look at him.

"You have to understand that Nate wasn't just my high school boyfriend. He was my parents' second child, basically. His parents are in business with mine, and our parents always said that I was going to end up with him. I believed that too. We got along really well in high school. I thought so, at least. Maybe not, now that I can look back at all of it."

Another pause. "I thought that we were going to end up together. We had talked about what we were going to name our kids." Nate wanted the most boring names. I'd wanted something fun, a Georgelle or something, but he always told me that was too hard for people to spell. I swallowed. "I mean, I was a communications major because I was going to work at our family business when we graduated from college. I spent half my weekends visiting him, but I thought all that time was worth it."

I shook my head. God, I had been such an idiot, believing all of that. I'd convinced myself that it was normal that I spent the weekends alone in his room at his campus, waiting for him to come back and hang out with me. I thought I was being supportive. I swallowed and kept talking. "And then, after one of my trips back to campus, I started noticing that something felt off. This is so gross to tell you, but I knew that I had a STD of some kind."

I closed my eyes against the memories that were coming back. Walking out of the bathroom, Spencer asking me if I felt okay, me telling her there was something up. "I went with Spence to the school clinic to figure out what was going on. And the nurse there told me what it was, without talking around it at all. I had herpes. And I hadn't gotten it from a toilet seat."

"Fuck." The word came bursting out of Lucas's mouth, and I turned back towards him. His shoulders were tensed up around his neck, and he was staring out at the street.

"So I knew. He'd been cheating on me." It was like I was back in the room with the nurse. I could remember every part of it. I'd been hungry because all I'd had was a bag of pistachios Spencer had stolen from the physics library, and I was feeling a little light headed. I was sitting in that plastic chair, sticking to it slightly, wondering how quickly I could get antibiotics and get on with things. I had a quiz the next day that I needed to study for.

The nurse was in purple scrubs with little flowers on them. She looked too cheerful to be saying what she was, telling me that the two tests couldn't be wrong. It wasn't a false positive.

"And the worst part was that I knew it. I knew it from the minute it all started. It wasn't like it had been one time, either. It had been for years. Since he went to college, basically. And the only reason that it had happened was that he had decided he didn't feel like using condoms."

"That piece of shit." Lucas's hands tensed into fists.

"I know. And the worst part was that he didn't even try to deny it. He just shrugged and asked me what I expected while we were in college. Like I was going to just forgive him. I just stopped talking to him. I didn't know what else to do, because he didn't have a reason for hurting me, really. Just that he wanted it, and I didn't matter to him. Everything that I had sacrificed to keep us going didn't matter to him."

A tear started to creep out of my eye, and I blinked it back. "Spencer and Raleigh were the only people who helped me during it. I couldn't even go to the doctor on my parents' insurance, because they were going to get the bill. I had to find a place that would take cash before I could get treated."

I could remember Spencer's face when I'd told her. She'd looked me directly in the eyes, then visibly swallowed. I knew now that she was holding back, that she wanted to tell me that it meant that Nate was cheating, and that she'd known that for a long time. She'd decided to let me find that out myself, where I couldn't deny it. "I'm going to look up a place that will let you pay cash. And it doesn't matter if it's far, because we'll take Lazzie. I'll find the duct tape. You just make yourself coffee now, okay?"

"You didn't tell your parents?" Lucas asked. His hand reached towards mine in the space between us, but he didn't reach any closer.

"You don't understand my parents. They have a very clear vision for what they want from me. As long as I've been alive, it's been for me to marry Nate and inherit the business. They think I need to get over this phase and get back together with Nate. Their concern is whether Nate would still take me back."

"Are you kidding?" Lucas's voice was low and threatening.

I shrugged, as much as I could manage. I still couldn't pretend that it didn't hurt. "Nate told my parents something about me not being in the right place for a relationship. My parents blame me for it. I should have transferred schools to be closer to him, or gone home on the weekends more, or whatever. That

I needed to focus on my future more and not be so selfish." I twisted the hair tie around my wrist into a knot in my hand. "I can't talk to them any more. I can't do anything, because they talk about it all the time. If I go home, it'll be about Nate and why I should have fixed things up. That I've failed by not being with him."

"I'm so sorry," he said, turning towards me. His eyes were soft and staring directly into mine. "That is shitty."

I nodded. "I had some things that reminded me of him today, and it spiraled into a panic attack. That's why I'm here."

"That's nothing to be ashamed of," he said quickly. "You're really brave for going through all of them."

If he thought that I was brave, I could be brave for another few seconds. "I like you. Like, I like you in a romantic way."

"You do?" His entire face broke into a smile. "Seriously?"

I ran a hand over my face, glancing down at the roof. It was like I couldn't not smile when he was smiling at me. "Seriously. I wasn't running away from you. I'm nervous and scared, but I really like you."

"Can I give you a hug now?" he asked, looking towards me. I nodded, and he scooted over towards me, wrapping me in his arms. I closed my eyes and leaned into his chest. I could feel his heartbeat, slow and steady.

And then, I turned around in his arms and kissed him.

Lucas's mouth met mine immediately. His arms tightened around me, and I closed my arms, leaning further into him. Drinking up all of him, everything that I could get.

The new start that I had been waiting for. This was it.

"Damn it, Arielle," he whispered, pulling me closer. "I've wanted you for so long."

"So long?" I whispered back, my mouth barely pulling away from his. We paused for a second and I pressed back into him. His hands started to run up my back.

"I've liked you since the day I met you. But you were – you weren't single. I would have been so happy to just be your friend, because I want you in my life, no matter how, but this is better," he replied. He pulled back just enough to tuck a piece of hair behind my ear, then stopped. "You have goosebumps."

I hadn't noticed. Despite the fact that it was February and we were sitting outside, something about the thrill of Lucas being here was keeping me warm. This was everything I needed, the fresh start I'd been waiting for without even knowing it. "I'm cold."

"Do you – " He ran a hand through his hair. "I

don't want this to sound too forward, but do you want to come back to my place?"

My heart started pounding at the idea. "Only if you make me hot chocolate."

He grinned down at me, his face beaming out into the night. "I'll do that. Let's go."

Chapter 16

The drive to Lucas's house felt like it took ages.

Part of me wanted to fill the silence, asking questions like *what are we* and *where are we going emotionally with all of this* and *wow I really like you, I should have said something sooner.*

But my brain was finally quiet. Like the right thing that had finally happened, and I knew it.

He parked the car in the garage, and I stared at him for a second. My brain had gone into hyperdrive again. I caught myself breaking into one giant, goofy smile before I followed him out of the car and up the steps into the house.

Lucas stopped in the entryway, hanging up his keys. I stopped and watched him. I was standing in Lucas's house, and there was only one reason that I had come here.

And I wanted that reason. I wanted to be here.

"Hey," he said, the corner of his mouth twitching upward. He took a step towards me.

"Hey," I said back, my voice small. I glanced down at the ground, then back up at Lucas.

"Your hair doesn't seem to be staying in place," he said, reaching out and tucking a piece of hair behind my ear.

"Yeah, I know," I said, glancing back down at the ground. My throat suddenly felt dry, and my pulse was racing. And it was cliché to say, but it was like there was a fire in my stomach. An actual physical response to having Lucas so close.

"So you want to take me up on that hot chocolate?" he said, taking a step closer to me.

"I – " *I want your hands on me.* I stared down at his hands, his fingers playing with his sleeve. I wanted to grab them and have them on me, not over there.

Oh god, I was actually thinking this. I was in for it.

"What were you saying?" he asked, taking another step towards me.

My brain had suddenly gone blank. "I think maybe we could skip the hot chocolate," I said, the words getting caught in my throat.

"What are you thinking instead?" he asked. His hand started to run up my side, and I closed my eyes. I leaned into him, pressing my face into his shoulder.

His hands ran up my side, and my entire body seemed to break out in goosebumps. This time it was from excitement, not cold. I tilted my head up and looked up at him.

"Can I kiss you again?" he asked, his hands still lightly touching my side. Lightly enough that I wasn't even sure if he was actually doing it, or if all of this was just an amazing dream that I was having.

"Yes," I said. And I stood up on my tiptoes and pressed my lips onto his.

He sighed into my mouth, his lips pressing against mine. It was like nothing else mattered at the moment, just him and me. That there were no more walls between us.

His other hand moved onto my back, and he lifted me slightly up. He held me tight, deepening the kiss as he walked back towards the kitchen stools. I tightened my arms around him. If I had felt excited before, it was almost like I felt honored now. Something precious.

He bit my lower lip as he set me down on the stool. I reached my arm around his back and pulled him closer again. It was as though I'd lost control of my body, that all I wanted was him. He was standing in front of me, too far away. I curled a leg around his body. He set one hand on the kitchen counter behind me and wrapped the other one around my back, pulling me closer and closer to him.

"I have been hoping for this since the day I met you," he said, pulling back for a second. "And after you kissed me in that bathroom, I couldn't stop thinking about it, Arielle."

I loved how he used my full name, like it was something magical. Something that he had to honor and keep for himself. The way he drew it out into a full three syllables, like he couldn't get enough of it. He sighed, his forehead coming to rest against mine. "I wanted you so badly that I couldn't – I didn't want to kiss you and know what it was like if you weren't interested. Because I knew the minute I kissed you, I wouldn't stop thinking about it."

I ran my fingers around his lips again. "And I wanted you to want me back," he said.

It was something about that. Lucas wanted me to pick him. He didn't want me to take him as the default option, because my friends or my parents or whoever thought I should. He wanted me, the Arielle I'd found and started to love, to pick him back.

I pulled him closer to me. "I want you."

He let out a groan, his hands tightening on my body. He pressed closer to me, and I ran my hand under the seam of his shirt. His skin was warm, his muscles tense. He groaned again, his teeth playing with my lower lip.

He loosened my legs around him, pushing them gently to the side. He ran a hand on the inside of my thighs, pushing up the dress I'd worn to the party. I arched my back towards his touch.

"This okay?" he whispered, into my ear, his lips starting to work a trail down my neck.

"God, yes, please." The words were a plea. I needed more. More of him, more of this.

His lips were on my collarbone now, and he nipped my skin. I groaned, the anticipation running through my body. I pressed my back against the counter and arched my back again, trying to get closer to him.

His fingers skimmed over the crease between my leg and my hip. I groaned again, louder this time. "Sorry," I whispered, biting my lip.

"Don't you dare apologize," he whispered, pressing his lips to my neck again. "I love it when you make that sound. I want to hear you, Arielle."

"I want you."

He knelt on the kitchen floor in front of me. He kissed the inside of my thigh, and I pressed my back against the counter again, trying to get closer to him. "Can I?"

"Please, oh god, please." The words weren't even said, they were whispered.

He kissed the inside of my thighs, getting closer and closer to where I wanted him, and I pressed up towards him. He gently bit the inside of my thigh, and I caught myself gasping. It was like he knew everything I wanted without me even knowing it myself.

"Lucas." I buried my hands in his hair, trying to

get him closer. I wanted him. Now, not making me wait.

"I waited three years for this. You can't make me rush," he said, grinning up at me. One of his fingers ran gently over my clit, and I almost jumped out of my seat. "I want you to enjoy this, and I want to know that you enjoy it."

God, this was so much. He kissed the inside of my thighs, all around where I wanted his mouth. I pushed back into him, wanting more, needing more. He skimmed his fingers over and around, and I screwed my eyes shut, not able to focus on anything else.

And then, he finally gave me what I needed. His tongue touched my clit, running in circles around it, and I dug my hands into his shoulders. My knuckles were white, and I felt it building inside me. My legs started to tremble, and I clung to him harder and harder. "Lucas. I need you inside of me. Please."

And then, I felt his fingers slide inside of me. I pressed myself up towards him, up towards his palm. He pulled them back slightly, and I grunted in frustration, pushing back towards him. "Oh god, please, Lucas."

"Say my name again," he said, looking up at me.

"Lucas," I whispered. He ran his tongue back over my clit. His fingers pressed slightly further into me, and then out, and I moaned, pressing back up into him.

His mouth started to work again, and threw my

head back. It was here. I needed him. "Please," I whispered again.

And this time, he gave me what I wanted. His fingers pressed inside of me, and the orgasm overtook me. I let out a noise that wasn't like anything I'd heard before. He stood up, his fingers beside me still, and tightened another arm around me.

I moaned, closing my eyes against all of the feelings. "Look at me," he said, his face hovering above mine. "Arielle, look at me."

I looped my trembling legs around him. My breathing was still fast and ragged, and I stared up at him. God, he was so beautiful. "Lucas."

The waves were coming more slowly now, and my breathing started to settle. I reached up and rested my hand on his cheek. "God. Lucas, that was so good."

He leaned down and kissed me, his tongue tracing around my lips again. "That was the hottest thing I've ever done. I would go down on you all day. I want to make you make that noise over and over again."

I tilted my head back and pressed my lips onto his again. He slid his fingers out of me, and I missed the feeling of him immediately. That I would have kept him there knowing that he was in me, that we couldn't be taken apart. "Should we try a round two?"

And just like that, my body was ready to go again. "Yes," I said, kissing him again.

He picked me up and set me on the ground in

front of him. He took a step back and stared at me for a second. "Arielle Mack, you are so hot."

I stared at him for a second. He stared back at me, visibly swallowing. "I cannot wait to get that dress off of you."

"Tell me what you want," I said, the words almost a whisper. I didn't know how I was brave enough to say it, but something about him made it possible. "Tell me what you want to do."

He took a step closer. "I want to take you upstairs, and I want to take this dress off. Slowly, so I can enjoy watching all of it." He ran his hand across my collarbone, and I shivered. "And then I want to have you in every way that I can. And I want to watch it the whole time. I want you to want me back, Arielle."

"You want me to tell you that I want it?" I asked back. I took another step towards him, almost in his arms now. I couldn't do anything but stare up at him, just wanting to watch his eyes.

"Tell me," he said, his hands running up and down my sides. "Tell me that you want me. That this feels good."

I would tell him that all day long. "I want you, Lucas."

And with that, he reached around and picked me up. "I'm not wasting a second," he said, tightening his grip around me as he carried me up the stairs.

He might have said that he wanted to take off my dress slowly, but by the time that we reached the bedroom, we had both lost patience with the idea of slowly. I wanted to feel him, and I wanted it now. We'd waited too long already.

He slammed the door to the bedroom shut with his room, almost running over towards the bed. I tumbled onto it, and pulled him closer to me. He climbed up onto the bed, almost on top of me. He reached down and pulled my dress off, and my hands went to the button of his shirt.

God, he actually had a perfect body. He was muscular, but not too muscular, the kind of person who could rescue you from a burning building.

"Let me get a condom," he said, kissing me again, and then reaching over for his nightstand. He came back and paused for a second. "You have no idea how amazing you look."

I stared back at him. "Are you going to just stare at me?"

He let out a groan, tearing open the condom package. He rolled back over and propped himself up on top of me. He reached up, his fingers pressing away more hair that had fallen in my face. "Look at me," he said, reaching down and kissing me gently.

And then, without looking away, he pressed in on me. He was bigger than I expected, and I gasped, pressing myself up towards him. It was as though all of me was filled with all of Lucas, that there was nothing left separately between the two of us.

He stayed still for a second, and I breathed. The

feeling of him instead of me was so much, so over-whelming, that I couldn't ask for more. And then, he moved back slightly, and I pressed my hips towards him. And like he knew what I wanted, he pressed all the way into me. I moaned, my fingers digging into his shoulder.

"You are amazing, Arielle," he said, his eyes still not leaving mine as he moved his hips back slightly, then back into me. I moaned again, pressing up towards him. "You are the most incredible person. Just like this. Just how you are.."

That was what I had wanted to hear. I was perfect as I was. I didn't need to change for him. I pulled him closer to me, still not tearing my eyes away from him, still wanting him.

He pressed into me again. "God, Lucas," I breathed.

As soon as I said his name, he sped up, his move-ments more urgent now. Like we couldn't get close enough to each other, that there would never be enough in between us. That we needed all of this. I dug my fingers into his back. It had never felt this good before.

I pressed my hips up towards him, and he groaned again, pushing back into me. Our bodies crashed together, and I pressed up and into him again. His movements were faster, his breathing heavier. I could feel his pulse racing through his chest.

"Arielle. *Arielle.*"

It was like my name was a plea, a prayer, something magical. He pressed into me again, his hands wrapping around my face. His eyes never left mine as he shuddered, closing his eyes for a second and then staring back at mine. "Wow."

"Wow," I repeated, my hand running up towards his hair and wrapping strands around my fingers.

He rolled over and propped himself up on his elbows, looking down at me. "We should have done that sooner." The corner of his mouth turned up into a smile as he looked at me again, his hand running over my side.

"You could be right," I replied, looking up at him. "Go get rid of the condom."

He started to roll over, then stopped to look at me. "Don't you dare move. I want to look at you like this."

"Sweaty and out of breath?" I asked.

He reached over and pushed a piece of hair back from my face. "Just – beautiful."

My breath caught in my throat again, and he reached down and kissed my forehead. "I'd be honored if you spent the night."

Chapter 17

I opened the door to the apartment to see Spencer staring at me.

"Hi," I said, unfastening the jacket that I had borrowed from Lucas and setting it down on the couch beside me.

She shifted her legs on the couch and stared at me even harder. I had not been expecting her to be this awake early. "Are you going to explain where you were last night? Or am I going to have to drag the story out of you?" she asked.

I was in for it now. "What do you mean?" I felt the nasty rush of adrenaline through me. I wasn't sure that I was quite ready to tell this story to everyone yet.

"You weren't here this morning when I got back," she said, crossing her arms. "And it clearly wasn't that you had been here and gone out to pick up breakfast for the two of us or something, because the light was on in our room, and there was stuff all over your bed."

Oh shit. I hadn't even thought about that. Of course Spencer was going to beat me home. Because she wasn't with Lucas, who had woken up and insisted that he bring me an espresso in bed. Which had of course led to more. "I – "

"I already pulled out the coffeemaker and made coffee. So you can sit down on the couch over there and explain exactly what happened," she said, patting the seat next to her.

I wasn't getting out of this. I sat down on the couch and she brought over a cup of coffee, handing it to me. I took a long sip. She was still staring at me. "Are you going to start talking, or am I going to have to resort to more serious strategies?"

"What are the more serious strategies?" I hadn't slept much last night, and more coffee was helping, at least.

She stared at me over the top of her coffee cup. "You asking that question is an attempted distraction strategy from you telling me what happened last night." She paused, then tilted her head to her side. "But theoretically, I may have downloaded several Athena Brigette audiobooks this morning, and theoretically, they may be on my phone, hooked up to a speaker that you can't reach, and ready to play for the entire day until you break down and tell me."

Oh no. I didn't want to hear my own terrible writing over and over again. And she'd probably downloaded the highest rated ones, and I wasn't listening to *His Lady of the Manor* again. "Okay. I'll talk."

She smirked. There was no other way to describe it. I took a deep breath. "So I may have hooked up with Lucas last night."

"I knew it!" She fist pumped so vigorously that her coffee splashed out of her cup and onto the couch. She glanced down at it. "Oops. But finally! The sexual tension has been killing me."

"The sexual tension has been killing *you*?"

"I mean, yeah. It's awful having to be in the room with two people who clearly just want to bang each other but have no idea how to make the first move. It's actually painful. Would not recommend it." She stared at me, narrowing her eyes. "It wasn't bad, right?"

"What do you mean?" I stared down at the surface of my coffee. I wasn't even sure that I wanted it any more, because my stomach had started to churn.

"You've been moping about the asshole for so long that I wasn't sure if you were going to be into a new person. It's the first time that I've hooked up with someone who isn't that asshole, so there's the whole learning curve again."

"It wasn't – it wasn't bad. Not like that," I said,

shaking my head. My hands tightened around the coffee cup at the memory.

She stared at me for a second and then burst out laughing. "Oh my god, Arielle. It was that kind of good. You don't even want to know the color that your face is right now. God, you have no idea how happy this makes me."

"It makes you happy that I hooked up with Lucas last night?" He was one of our friends. I could have ruined everything with a thoughtless rebound. I could have made it awkward with our entire friend group.

"Yes!" She set the coffee down on the table, probably so she wouldn't ruin the rest of the couch with coffee stains. "You've been wallowing. Lucas is great. He's fun, he's smart, he's a good guy. If I were going to build a guy for you from scratch, it would be Lucas."

"You're not supposed to pick people for me. I think I'm supposed to pick people on my own," I shot back.

"I'm ignoring everything you say right now, just so you know." She grinned at me again, leaning forward and giving me a hug. "I'm so happy for you. This has been so long in the making."

It was hard for me to deny that I was happy, too. That I was actually thrilled that I had been over with Lucas, that we had slept together, that I had gotten to make fancy coffee this morning.

"I'm scared that I'm not scared," I said, my voice

coming out smaller than I had expected. "This sounds stupid as I'm saying it. I feel super happy about what happened, but at the same time, scared that I'm happy?"

"I mean, that makes sense." Spencer scooted onto the couch next to me. "You were with that person for a pretty long time, so of course, you're going to feel weird about jumping back into something. I'd almost be more surprised if you weren't feeling slightly off about it."

I swallowed. She was right, but knowing that she was right didn't make it easier. "It's taken me a while to be Arielle again. I don't want to turn back into somebody who's totally defined by her relationship."

"Are you kidding?" She shook her head. "Lucas is nothing like that asshole. He likes you for you, and he doesn't want you to change into some Stepford house-wife. And you know who Arielle is, and you're not going to lose that just because you like a guy."

"I know." I had to listen to Spencer, not to the voice in the back of my head. I wasn't letting Nate's ghost steal this from me.

"This isn't the same thing at all. I can tell you that. And you should just see what happens." She shrugged, picking her coffee cup back up. "And you know what? If things go wrong, we will deal with it together. If you're going to get your heart broken, isn't it better to do it with your best friends?"

"That wasn't that much help last time." There

hadn't been drinking, because I was on some pretty strong antibiotics.

"I object. Things were a hundred percent better because you had me and Raleigh. Imagine if you'd had to do all of that alone," she said.

That was true. I wouldn't have even been able to find a clinic without their support. "You guys really are the best," I said finally, reaching forward and giving her a hug.

She grinned and hugged me back, eventually leaning back and smiling. "I know. Now, are you going to buy me breakfast today? Because I should also point out that I cleaned up the apartment this morning, and you owe me one."

"CAN I have two egg sandwiches and a vanilla latte?" I asked, digging through my wallet at the coffee shop next to campus.

It was the Wednesday after our party, but I was still getting lunch for Spencer. Cleaning up the apartment after a party was an endeavor, not something to be taken lightly. She'd done all of that while I'd had fun with Lucas, so I still owed her.

The barista passed me my drink, and I tucked the egg sandwiches into my bag. I'd stop by the lab and give Spencer hers later.

Lilith waved as I walked out of the cafe and

towards the classroom for senior seminar. "Ready for today?"

We were getting the votes in for our senior presentations, and I was not looking forward to this. A big part of me wanted to skip it, but the dean's office had advised me to keep going to the class while my complaint was processing. I was more likely to be taken seriously if it looked like I wasn't just using the complaint to get out of class.

That was ridiculous, in my opinion, but I wasn't going to jeopardize the complaint. "At least it doesn't matter if we fail," I said, trying to keep my voice light. I might not need the class, but nobody liked to fail.

"We can go out afterwards and forget about it," she said. We walked into the building and then into the classroom auditorium, taking seats towards the back. I sat behind the tallest person in class so that I didn't have to make eye contact with Professor Jenkins.

I looked over at her as Professor Jenkins walked to the front of the room, and she grimaced. He cleared his throat at the front of the room. "We're going to do this like an actual presentation, where you can see live feedback. My assistant has tallied up the votes from all of you, both for the best and for the worst presentation. As a reminder, if you come in first, you will be guaranteed an A. If you come in last, you will fail this presentation."

"Why does he do this?" Lilith whispered to me. "This is bad enough already."

"I know," I whispered back. It was mean enough to make it a popularity contest, without the threat of failing the project.

Professor Jenkins turned on the screen. All of our names came up, and he pressed a button on his computer. "And here we have our winners and losers," he announced, gesturing towards the screen.

I wanted to close my eyes, but I forced myself to look. Lilith and I were on the screen on the bottom. The bar next to our name kept going slightly up as the votes rolled in.

Wait. We weren't actually going to lose this. We weren't going to fail.

I looked again. Our bar was actually pulling ahead. More and more of the votes were showing up on the screen, and more and more of them were going to us.

Lilith looked at me, and I looked back at her. This couldn't be real.

The screen stopped, and a box appeared in front of our names. Professor Jenkins stared up at the screen, his mouth dropping. "The winners are – "

I was just going to wait for this, to hear our names. "Lilith and Arielle," he said, almost spitting it out.

Lilith leaned over and wrapped me into a giant hug. "Yes!"

"Well, those two will get an A," he said. His voice

left no doubt what he thought about that. "Now that we've heard that some of you are also social justice warriors, let's move onto class."

I shook my head back to Lilith. We'd done it. We'd stood up for what we believed in.

"What a good start to reading period," she whispered back to me, and I gave her a high five.

Chapter 18

The high from Professor Jenkins's defeat lasted me all the way until I got back to my apartment to pack for reading period. I sat down on the couch and opened my email to find that Margaret had sent me back the detailed comments on *The Lord Who Loved Me*. They were rough, to put it nicely.

The problem was that as much as I wanted to hate Margaret, she'd actually given me really good feedback. Now that I was reading it again, I realized that all of her criticisms were right. The characters were flat, and I didn't understand why my female lead was so resistant to the idea of a relationship with the male lead.

I wanted to hate her, but she was actually a much better editor than Emma was.

I might have to scrap all of this and rewrite it. If I

was going to write a book about how I wanted a healthier relationship model than what I'd had with Nate, this wasn't it. Not by a long shot.

"Are you packed?" Spencer asked, coming into the living room and clearing her throat. "Earth to Arielle."

I looked up from my computer, momentarily lost in thought. "Packed?"

"For the weekend?" She tossed a throw pillow towards me. "Come on, Ari. You were the one who was the most excited about this weekend."

"You're the one who's most excited," I replied, sticking my tongue out at her. But I shut my computer and stuffed it into my backpack. We had Thursday and Friday off from school this week to prepare for midterms, but since it was senior year, we'd rented a house on a nearby lake with our friends.

My phone buzzed, and I picked it up. From Lucas, *Do you and Spence want me to drive?*

"Lucas wants to know if you want him to drive us," I said, choosing to ignore Spencer's original questions about whether I had packed.

"I don't think we want to take Lazzie, so yes. But fair warning, I don't have to watch you two, and I will make comments if you get too cutesy." She glanced towards me over her shoulder as she got snacks down from the cabinet. "Put your laptop away, and start packing. I want to get out of here."

My phone buzzed again. *And just so you know, Lilyanna is riding with me.* "Lucas is bringing Lilyanna." God, even saying his name sent a little bit of joy through me. *That's my Lucas!* said the voice in the back of my head.

"Okay, we're totally driving with him then. I love that dog." Spencer plopped down on the side of her bed and stared at me. "Put your damn things in your damn bag, Arielle. I want to get out of here and start enjoying my weekend."

"I have to work this weekend," I said, shoving my laptop into my bag. Now I had to pick clothes, which was the much tougher part. Now that I'd actually hooked up with Lucas, part of my brain wanted to make sure that he only saw me in my cutest clothes. Which didn't even make sense, because now he'd seen me naked.

Nope, I was stopping this line of thinking before I turned bright red. I cleared my throat, turning towards Spence. "Don't give me crap about this. I have something big due for work."

"You're the one who made a big deal about how badly you needed a break. So hush and pack." She threw a shirt at me. "That's yours."

"Thanks," I stuffed it into my bag without looking. Spencer was clearly going to start packing for me if I didn't get a move on.

I finished stuffing things into my bag as the doorbell rang. "Can you get that?" Spencer called from the bathroom.

I jogged to the door and opened it. Lucas was standing outside, his hands stuffed into his pockets and his hair messy. His car was parked on the street behind him, Lilyanna hanging her head out the window. "Hey," he said, a giant smile breaking out as he looked at me. "You look great."

"Thanks," I said, turning bright red. I glanced down at my outfit, which was a giant sweater and comfy tights, perfect for a drive but not for impressing people. "I mean, I'm not dressed up."

"Yeah, but you still look great," he replied, taking a step forward, and pulling me into a hug. His head rested on top of mine for a second, and I could feel him sigh before he released me. "Are you two ready for the drive?"

"We might still be packing," I said, trying to make the *we* sound as convincing as possible.

"We are not still packing," Spencer's voice came from inside the apartment, and then I felt a bag drop onto my feet. "You're welcome. I finished making sure that all of your things were in the bag. And don't worry, I remembered the condoms."

She was lucky she was one of my best friends, or I'd have to kill her. My face turned an even brighter red, and Lucas looked down at the ground before he awkwardly cleared his throat. "Planning a big weekend, Spence?"

"It just always pays to be prepared, right?" She smirked at me, then spotted Lilyanna. "Oh, you're the cutest!"

"I can't believe that Raleigh let us take Lilyanna for the weekend," I said, picking up my bag and walking towards the car. Lucas opened the trunk, and I threw in my bag, followed by Spencer's.

"To be clear, they're letting *me* take Lilyanna. I don't know if Raleigh trusted the rest of you to have the dog for the weekend. She'd probably come back to a Lilyanna ten pounds heavier from table scraps." His hand pressed into my back for a second. He slipped on sunglasses for the drive, and I thought my heart might jump out of my chest. God, he was so attractive.

"They totally trust me with Lilyanna," I said, walking around to the passenger seat. Spencer had already claimed the backseat and was playing tug of war with Lilyanna. Lucas didn't seem at all concerned that Lilyanna was shedding all over his car, which only made me like him more.

"Sometimes you say these things, and I don't think you even believe what you're saying," he replied, leaning over and brushing a piece of hair out of my face. My heart skipped a beat. "You've clearly never had a dog."

"My parents weren't really dog people." My parents didn't like anything that was going to make a mess in the house and not arrive perfectly trained.

"The important thing is that Raleigh still trusts me with her dog for the weekend," he replied, walking around to the drivers' side and opening the door. I walked around to my side of the car and slipped into the passenger seat.

"Who's the cutest? You're the cutest," Spencer cooed from the backseat, rubbing Lilyanna's head. "The best dog in the whole wide world. Yes, you are!"

"Spence, this might be the only time that I've seen you be cuddly," Lucas said from the front seat. He leaned forward and turned on the car, stretching the seatbelt across his chest.

Which I noticed too much. Because putting on your seatbelt was not supposed to be seductive. There was nothing sexy about not wanting to die in a car crash.

Lucas turned towards me, looking down at the stereo. "Driver gets music rights, just in case you've forgotten that."

"Don't even think about listening to that acoustic crap that you normally listen to," Spencer said, pausing from petting and turning towards Lucas. "I refuse to spend the next three hours of my life listening to a bunch of men whine about their problems over a sad guitar."

"It seems like you have strong preferences when it comes to music," Lucas replied. He pulled out of the parking spot and started the drive down our street towards the highway.

"My preference," she replied, leaning forward and crossing her arms, "is that I don't want to listen to shitty things for the entire drive. I didn't know that you were going to turn that into a controversial opinion."

"You think all singer songwriters are whiny?" Lucas asked, his fingers drumming on the steering wheel.

"Of course not!" Lilyanna nudged Spencer, and she turned back towards the dog for a second. "You're the cutest. The absolute cutest. Anyway, Lucas, I think that the men who write acoustic music about how they can't get laid are whiny. That has nothing to do with being profound. Taylor Swift totally got a bad rap for that."

"She did get a bad rap. It was completely unfair," I said. "I mean, everyone talked all about how she just wrote music about guys, but then, there are all these male artists who just write songs about women. And nobody ever accuses them of being shallow for it."

"It's classic. Dismissing women's contributions because they're women. Thinking that because something is about relationships, it can't be deep and meaningful unless it comes from a man," Spencer said, uncrossing her arms to pet Lilyanna for a second. "You're the cutest dog. You're so cute."

"It's so true." Beyond true. "You only have to look at literature for an example. Did you know that the

New York Times book review does fewer than five romance novels each year? Because they're not considered real literature. And that's even though most of the books sold in this country are genre fiction, and the majority of that is in romance. Because romance is often written for women by women, it gets dismissed as something that's less than all of the other things that get written."

"Do you have strong feelings about romance novels?" Lucas asked, turning to look at me for a second before refocusing on the road.

Spencer snorted from the backset, then covered it up by cooing at Lilyanna. "Yes!" I said. Very strong feelings, in fact. "Romance novels are actually some of the most revolutionary books out there. Think about it. You have the chance to write out what women really want. For example, in Pride and Preju-dice, you see concepts about consent way ahead of their time."

"Continue," Lucas said, as though I needed any help with that. I could talk about this for days.

"I will, but not because you told me to!" Just in case there was any doubt on that point. "The whole reason that women like Mr. Darcy so much is that he tells Elizabeth I want you, but if you don't want me, I'll leave. I'm not entitled to have you just because I'm rich and have a penis. He's basically asking for consent to keep chasing her. And that's why so many women love that book." I took a deep breath, out of breath from talking so fast. "The problem is that society has then turned it into this thing where it's like, women must like him because he's rich and brooding and wants to marry her. And she's so undesirable because she's smart. Which is not at all the case. It's a revolutionary feminist tale by Victorian standards!"

"You can't argue with Arielle on this," Spencer chimed in, leaning forward again. "She's an expert."

"I'm not even that much of an expert. I just get tired of people trying to talk down this kind of stuff because women wrote it. It's like how JK Rowling published under her initials because she thought that she'd be taken more seriously. There are all these men who just write about how they can't get laid and call it literature. Have they ever considered that maybe if they weren't assholes, people would want to sleep with them?"

"So you're saying that you have a strict no asshole policy," Lucas said, tapping his fingers on the wheel.

"Only metaphorically," Spencer interrupted. "Arielle's not a kink shamer. If you're into butt stuff –
"

She was definitely sitting in the back seat so that I couldn't turn around and punch her. Lucas snorted. "I don't think she was expecting you to say that."

"I just felt like I needed to stand up for my friends here. I didn't want you to get the wrong impression about our dear friend Arielle," Spence replied, grinning at me. I gave her the finger.

She was definitely just picking on me now. I was the kind of person who would turn red and get embarrassed about this stuff, and Spence knew it. Writing romance novels didn't mean that I didn't get embarrassed about what I was thinking about. I was glad that I wrote Regency, because I got to skip the part where I put my admittedly pretty vanilla sex fantasies down on paper.

"I don't think I have the wrong impression of Arielle," he replied, which was about the worst thing that he could have said.

Spencer snorted so loudly that she startled Lilyanna, who started to bark at the window. "Sorry, babe," Spencer said, leaning over and petting her. "That wasn't aimed at you."

Of course she would apologize to Lilyanna before she would apologize to me. I shook my head at her, and she just shrugged back at me.

"I'm going to pick the music for the trip," I said, raising my voice to make it clear that the earlier conversation was over. "If you all have preferences – "

"It's probably not going to be what you want to listen to," Lucas said, glancing over at me. My stomach flipped. He was literally preemptively making fun of my taste in music and part of me thought that was cute. I was in for it.

"I can pick the music if you two can't agree on it," Spencer offered.

"As nice of an offer as that is, I'm pretty sure that I'm the driver, and that means that I get to pick the music," Lucas replied, glancing in between me and then back towards Spencer. "And don't you get too handsy with Lilyanna."

"Don't you get too handsy with Arielle," she snapped back, burying her face in Lilyanna's neck.

Lucas glanced towards me, raising an eyebrow. We hadn't talked about this, about what we were going to tell her friends. I didn't want to have that conversation yet, because I wasn't sure about the answer.

But there were friends where you couldn't hide anything, because they could read everything on your face. Even if I hadn't told Spencer what happened, she would have known the second that I walked through the door.

"I'm keeping both hands on the wheel," Lucas said, raising an eyebrow at me. My heart did another one of its little leaps in my chest.

Spencer shook her head and then buried her face in Lilyanna's fur. "This is going to be a long trip, isn't it."

It took another solid three and half hours of driving before we pulled up to the cabin. We might have gotten lost, but because I was the person who was supposed to be helping Lucas navigate, I didn't want to point that out. Luisa's car was already in the driveway, and she waved to us as we walked in.

"Did you all get lost? I thought you were leaving maybe five minutes after the rest of us," she said, glancing over from where she was unpacking grocery bags. "We even had time to run out and pick up snacks for the weekend."

"We absolutely did not get lost," I shot back, definitely too quickly. Lucas's hand drifted behind my back for a second, his thumb grazing along the top of my leggings.

"I definitely thought that we got lost," Spencer said, coming in the door with Lilyanna on a leash. Usually Lilyanna was good about not running off and chasing squirrels, but the squirrels here were real athletic squirrels, not fat campus squirrels.

"Well, you all can make sure that we have dinner prepared tonight." Luisa brushed her hands on her jeans and smiled at us. "I was thinking of taking a walk down to the lake. Does anyone want to come?"

I stared at the half full fridge, suddenly feeling guilty for being this late to the cabin. I should have been the person who watched the map more closely and made sure that we actually got here in time. And instead, my friends had actually gone and done all of the work to get the place ready for us while we had been lost on the road.

Not that that was entirely my fault. I just wasn't the best when it came to figuring out how to read the stupid instructions on the map. Spencer was one of those people who never got lost, and I was one of those people who got lost in New York where the streets were literally numbered. This might have been why she was a STEM major and I was a novelist.

"I think Lilyanna needs the walk, so I'm down to go," Spencer said, glancing around at the living room. "This place is beautiful, by the way."

"You can give the credit to Jason," she replied. "Spencer and Arielle, I saved the upstairs bedroom for you both. I'm in the little room next door, and the guys are downstairs. Lucas, sorry, you got the basement."

"I got the basement?" he asked, shifting his weight slightly from foot to foot.

She nodded. "We all called dibs on rooms when we were coming out, and since you weren't here, Tyler and Jason took the room with the best view. But you have your own room. It might have been a closet."

"I'm guessing that you gave us the same room and took the single because you know that we'll stay up talking," Spencer said to Luisa.

"I'm never sharing a room with you two again. When I want to go to sleep, I want to go to sleep. And you two can talk the whole night," Luisa replied, shaking her head. In our defense, that trip had been a time of deep emotional crisis for Spencer. One of her robots had started acting up two days before a robotics competition.

Lilyanna barked, and Spencer reached down and scratched her behind the ears. "I think this girl is ready to head out and take her walk."

"I'll finish putting away the groceries," I said, nodding towards the fridge.

"Thanks," Luisa said, heading upstairs.

I walked over to the fridge and bent down, pulling out a bag of chips and several things of salsa from the grocery bag. Luisa was one of those people who liked to eat more salsa than chips, and she was also very picky about the quality of her salsa. Which meant that she would often buy nine or ten jars, and then eat the first half of each before deciding that something else was better.

Honestly, my friends were all ridiculous, and I loved them for it.

"Need some help?" Lucas asked. He'd walked up behind me and was standing very close as I started to unload the bags of groceries. "Seems like this could be the kind of job that requires two people."

"I think I can manage to put the salsa in the fridge by myself," I replied, reaching into the bag and pulling out another jar.

"Are you sure?" he asked, his breath tickling my ear.

"We're heading out," Spencer called from the

back door. "Call me if you finish doing house chores and want to join."

"We might walk around the lake," Luisa called back. "It's a bit of a walk."

"Sounds good," Lucas called back. His hand drifted down to my side, and I leaned into him.

As soon as the back door closed, Lucas spun me around, taking me into his arms. Before I had the chance to kiss him, he'd already reached down and planted his lips on mine.

I took a step back into the fridge, closing my eyes for a second. God, this was all so good. Having Lucas here, being in his arms. Knowing that even when I left his arms, I'd still be surrounded by people who loved me.

"I wanted to do that for the whole drive up here," he said, lifting his lips off mine and looking down into my eyes. "The entire damn drive."

"Is that we got so lost?" I asked, tightening my arms around his back. "You were distracted?"

"Very distracted," he replied, running his hands through my hair. I closed my eyes and leaned into him again. He was here, and I was here, and that it was all going to be good.

"You know, they were planning to go for a long walk around the lake," he said, his hand starting to run up my side.

"That's right," I replied, swallowing, as though that was going to stop the heat building inside me.

"I think that we have lots of time if there are other things that we wanted to do other than put away salsa," he said again, his voice low. I actually shivered when I heard his voice. Shivered.

I reached up and wrapped my arms around his neck. "That doesn't seem like a bad idea at all."

He nuzzled the top of my head. "And I wouldn't mind seeing the view from your room. Or my room. Or any room."

I laughed and buried my face in his shoulder. "Let's go."

Chapter 19

"Do you think there's life on other planets?"

I glanced over towards Luisa, who was deep in conversation with Spencer. "I mean," Luisa continued, "you're our resident physics expert, so you should be able to answer this question without a problem."

"Taking quantum physics doesn't make me an expert on everything," Spencer replied, dunking a chip in salsa jar number two.

"But it means you know a lot more than the rest of us about this stuff." Luisa pulled up one of the blankets around her. We were sitting on the deck and looking out at the view. It was beautiful, but definitely colder than I had been expecting. Maybe not surprising, but I always thought of lakes as being like in Southern California, where it was sometimes sweatshirt weather but it was never really cold.

"Is this really the argument that we're having right now?" Tyler asked, walking outside with another of the many jars of salsa in hand. "And Luisa, why did we need three of the same salsa?"

"They're not the same. One is mild, one is medium, and one is spicy. And I wanted an actual mild salsa, but the problem is that most salsa companies make salsa for white people who live in the Midwest, so I got them all to make sure that I got the right one," Luisa replied.

"As a white person from the Midwest, I object to that statement," Jason said, reaching towards the middle and grabbing one of the chips.

"I took you out to the Thai place near campus, and you started crying into your pho," Luisa replied.

"That wasn't about the spice!" he said, stuffing a chip into his mouth. "You were making me watch sad cat videos on your phone."

"Luisa. That's not nice," Spencer said.

"All of this is fake news," she shot back. "I didn't make one of my friends cry on purpose. He brought it on himself asking for the extra spicy pho."

I leaned back, and Lucas raised an eyebrow at me. My heart did a bit of a flip, and I swallowed, not meeting his eyes exactly. It was so nice to be here with him, to be hanging out with everyone like this was a totally normal thing for all of us.

Nate had never liked my friends, but Lucas was

already one of them. It felt so easy and right to have him here with everyone.

"Does someone mind grabbing the water pitcher from inside?" Jason asked, not meeting any of our eyes. "This salsa is – you know. I think I might be allergic to something in it."

Of course. But I'd spare him anyway. "I'll get it." I was pretty sure that I felt my phone ringing in my pocket, and if it was my editor, I didn't want to answer it in front of everyone.

Lucas glanced up at me. "Need help?"

My heart fluttered again, but I shook my head. "I'll be good. I have to run to the bathroom anyway."

I pushed open the door to the house and walked in, the heat hitting me in the face. I missed the chill of the wind outside for a second. My phone trilled again. Worse than my editor, it was my parents. I was supposed to have answered them about that stupid party, and I'd been putting it off.

I stared at the phone for a second. There was no point in ignoring it. I was just going to get a passive aggressive voicemail reminding me that I was supposed to call them. I closed my eyes for a second, then looked down at the phone again. I had waited for long enough that the phone had made the decision for me.

I opened it and clicked on the voicemail. My mom's clipped voice came through the speaker. "Arielle. This is your mother." As though I was going to forget the voice of someone who I had had to live with for so many years. "You still haven't returned my calls about your father's birthday party. You are an adult, and I would expect that you would have the politeness to return my calls when I request it." Silence for a second. "Nate and his family have already replied that they will be in attendance."

The last person I wanted to see in the world was Nate. But of course that wasn't the answer that my family wanted. My parents wanted to hear that things were all better with Nate, that I was going to get back together with him and be the quiet, polite daughter who was happy being Nate's shadow. Be the person who was living the life that someone else wanted.

It had taken me long enough to figure out that what my parents wanted for me wasn't what was going to make me happy. I didn't want to be the person building my life around Nate.

My dreams were just as important as his. I wanted to write, I wanted to build a future where I wasn't working in the family business. I wanted to see what I could do, even if I failed.

But I had never told my parents that. Because there was no way that I was going to be able to explain it to them. My parents would have told me that I had to get over it, that I should realize how it was going to look, that things were already figured out. I was going to end up with Nate.

But that wasn't my problem now. I put my phone

back into my pocket, grabbing the water pitcher and heading back outside to my chosen family.

BACK ON THE PATIO, Luisa had picked up the argument about whether there was life on other planets again. Spencer started talking about how she wasn't a planetary biologist, which was an entirely different thing than being a robot builder with strong interests in quantum physics. Jason tried to insert himself into the conversation, then was reminded that he'd needed the water pitcher after eating the medium salsa.

We'd all split up after that to get ready for dinner and study for a couple hours. As much as we all wanted this to be a weekend away, there was the reality that we had these days off to prep for midterms. My grades didn't matter as much at this point, but everyone else was applying to graduate school.

I sat down on the bed in the room that I was sharing with Spencer. "A biologist. Seriously. Jason thought that I was a biologist," Spencer said, reaching into her suitcase.

For some reason, Spencer was finding this to be an insult. "In his defense, you do always seem to know everything related to space."

"You can like physics for reasons totally unrelated

to space!" She shook her head, her ponytail whipping back and forth. "How do you think that they got computer chips small enough to fit into a phone you can put in your pocket? Physicists. How do you think — "

"Physicists," I answered. Somehow, I was pretty sure I knew where she was going with this one.

"If you are enjoying any piece of technology in your life, you should thank a physicist." She sat down on her bed. "I feel the same way about physics that you feel about romance novels, and I am tired of people thinking that it's some kind of weird nerdy passion."

It was kind of a nerdy passion, but there was nothing wrong with that. "Yeah, but everyone thinks that it's so cool that you do physics, and everyone would think that I'm an airhead if they found out that I wrote romance novels."

"And yet you tell me all about how romance novels are so critically important to understand the human condition, and then you talk yourself down like this." She leaned her head to the side, still looking directly at me. "Am I detecting some internalized misogyny here?"

"I am not having this discussion with you right now," I said, leaning down and tossing a pair of socks at her head. "You are going to outsmart me, and then I'm going to end up having to admit you're right."

She grinned, leaning over and tossing the socks back towards me. "I'm going to take Lilyanna out for another walk. Do you want to come with me?"

I glanced out the window towards the lake. It had gotten dark, but it was still beautiful out. "Thanks but no thanks. I think I'm going to try to get through half a scene or so."

"I thought you claimed you needed a vacation," she said, standing up and rolling her shoulders.

"I know, but I need the time. These are tough comments, and it's going to take me a while to get through them all." I hadn't written a good novel, and I had to figure out how I was going to fix that. "But I'll do a double long walk tomorrow to make up for it."

She walked to the door and glanced back over her shoulder at me. "You don't have to apologize for it. I love walking Lilyanna. If I hadn't already chosen the coolest science of all time, I would have become a vet."

I snorted and reached for my headphones, tucking them into my ears. "Shut up and go walk the dog."

She vanished down the stairs, and I turned my attention to the computer screen in front of me. I was reaching the point of the novel where the lady was starting to fall for the lord who she had spurned for so long. Where she was realizing that she wanted something else.

That was it. She had to figure out who she was before she could fall for the lord. Until she knew herself, she couldn't fall in love with anyone else. That's what I had to show.

I stared down at the screen, starting to type. Once I realized that, everything fell into place. Margaret had told me what I needed to change, and now I just had to do it.

"What are you doing?"

I jumped, pushing my laptop back and sending it flying across the bed. "Lucas!"

"Did you just type the sentence, 'her heaving bosom betrayed a hint of her excitement'?" He was standing right over me, his head craned to see what I was doing.

"Why are you creeping on what I'm writing on my personal computer?"

"Sorry!" He held his hands up and backed onto Spencer's bed. "I was coming to say hi to you. And you didn't hear me because you had headphones in."

"So the most logical thing to do was to read what I was writing on my computer?" I asked, looking down.

"Not on purpose!" He ran a hand through his hair. "But you were typing so fast and so focused that I didn't want to startle you."

I closed my eyes for a second. I was going to make it through this. My heart was thudding still, and it seemed like thought was going to be the only way out of this.

I wasn't going to be able to talk around it without making it more obvious that I was hiding something. *And if he really cares about you, then he'll be excited. If you want Lucas to know the real Arielle, not the Arielle you made up for Nate, you have to tell him.*

Well then. "I write romance novels."

Lucas stared at me for a second, his head tilting towards the side. "For fun?"

Ugh. I hated that question. "Not just for fun. I'm a writer. Like a published writer."

"That's awesome!" His face lit up.

"Give me a second." I held up my hand and swallowed. It was so weird to be openly talking about this. "I work as a ghostwriter for a really famous romance author. She retired a while ago, and so I've been writing novels under her name since."

He sat down on the bed next to me and wrapped his arm around me. "Ari, are you kidding? That's awesome! I've never met a published author before."

Even though part of me had expected that he was going to think it was awesome, it was still so relieving to hear him say it. More proof that Lucas was a new beginning, a new chapter. I took another deep breath, my heart rate slowing. "That's why I care so much about romance." Now that the words were starting to come out, they were coming out in word vomit. "I want to write things that matter, you know? And I write a lot of books that I think matter, but I don't want people to dismiss them just because they're a genre that people think doesn't have anything to say."

He shook his head at me, leaning back and brushing a piece of hair off my face. "But can we talk about you for a second?"

I stopped and looked at him, tilting my head slightly. "About me?"

"How cool is it that you are an actual published writer? That you've been doing all of this and going to school and balancing everything?"

"It's just my job." I could feel myself starting to turn pink. Part of me was thrilled that he was so excited, and part of me found that it was too much. I'd gone from being secret about this to it being something people really cared about. I didn't know how to be in the spotlight all of a sudden.

"You can't say that writing books that people buy in airports all over the world is just a job." He grinned, reaching forward and wrapping me in a hug. "Arielle. You're awesome."

Now my heart rate was going to fly through the roof again, but in a good way. "I know. But I also try to treat it like a job. I have to pay for rent and school and everything, and I can't let myself get hung up on all the creative parts."

He leaned back, a hand still on my shoulder. "You're entirely funding college from your writing?"

I swallowed. "Not by choice. I want to graduate

without a ton of debt, and my parents refuse to pay for anything except the credit hours for communications." They'd told me that I could have the rest if I made the right decisions. But I knew what the right decisions were code for.

"That's terrible of them," he said, his hand tightening on my shoulder. "But I'm so proud of you, Arielle. So what author do I need to pick up?" His fingers were massaging my shoulder, and I leaned into him.

"Athena Brigette." I swallowed. "I've been ghostwriting for her for a pretty long time. Most of her stuff published in the past three years is mine."

"That's doubly awesome," he said, continuing to rub my shoulders. "You're not just writing for anyone. It's a big name, right?"

"She has rabid fan clubs. They will let me know if they think I'm not doing justice to their favorite author. Don't read the reviews." I had made that mistake once, and it had taken me weeks to start writing again.

Lucas laughed, leaning forward and kissing me on the forehead. "I don't need to read the reviews to know that you're a huge deal, Ari."

There was a noise outside my room, followed by Spencer's voice. "Don't eat that!"

"I'm guessing Lilyanna is back from her walk," Lucas said, reaching down and squeezing my hand.

He stood up and grinned down at me. "I should leave before Spencer gets back. And anyway, I've got some Athena Bridgette to go read." He leaned forward again, kissing me. "But again, Arielle. You're even more awesome than I knew. I'm so proud of you."

Chapter 20

Perhaps, she said, swishing her skirts around her ankles, *"you should consider sending me a letter in the morning. I suppose if your courier were to come to my home, I would not object."*

End of chapter, I typed, leaning back against the wall and looking down at my laptop.

It had been so long since I'd written something that I was really proud of. I'd forgotten what it was like to shut my laptop and feel the rush of having said something meaningful, not just put words on a page because I needed to hit a goal for the editors.

Spencer pushed open the door and sat down on the edge of the bed. "What are you still doing here?"

"Finishing stuff up," I said. Lucas had headed downstairs, but I wanted to finish up the chapter. It was almost writing itself.

"I thought the deal was that you weren't going to work the whole time that we're here," she said, trying to grab my laptop. "You're the one who told me I couldn't bring the robot!"

I dropped my closed laptop on my bed and pushed it under my pillow. "I'm done! Not working any more."

"I was hoping that you were going to tell me that you were continuing to plan your dramatic comeback against your asshole professor," Spencer said. "That would be the only acceptable kind of work to be doing on vacation. Revenge plotting."

"I think the fact that he has to give me an A because the class voted, and we won, is revenge enough," I replied. "You know that it killed him on the inside. All he wanted to do was to fail us, and the class said nope. It's the perfect revenge for his comments about people's weights."

"I can give you a whole rant on that if you want," she replied. "It's one of my favorite rants, about how people don't understand that the point of clothes is to protect you from the elements."

"I think I've heard that rant before," I said, standing up and stretching. I had definitely been writing for longer than I thought, and my back hurt from hunching over my laptop. "Want to grab snacks?"

We headed out into the kitchen. Lilyanna ran out to greet us, bounding in from the other room. "Are you the best girl?" Spencer cooed, leaning down and starting to rub her behind the ear.s "Yes, you are!"

"Should I be insulted that you said hi to Lilyanna before me?" Lucas asked, walking a few steps behind her. He must have just come back from a run, holding his t-shirt in his hands.

Focus, Arielle. I was not going to get carried away by all of the feelings that were going on in my head right now. I was going to focus on talking to Spencer. And Lucas.

Who really could put a shirt on so that I could focus better.

Almost like he knew what I was thinking, he took a few steps towards me, catching my eye and grinning. "What have you two been up to?"

"Arielle," Spencer said, using my full name so I knew this was a call out, "has been doing work."

"Work?" Lucas asked, raising an eyebrow slightly and taking another step towards me. I could smell the soap from the shower he must have taken. Brain, focus. "The fun parts of work or the boring parts?"

There are no sex scenes in the Lord Who Loved Me series, calm down, I started to say, then stopped myself. "Just a few things that I wanted to finish up. You know. Stuff."

"I told her it was only acceptable if she was plotting her revenge on the sexist asshole who calls himself a communications professor," Spencer said. She was now completely crouched down next to Lilyanna, rubbing her fur. "Who's the best girl?"

"I was going to go for a walk around the lake,"

Lucas said. Lilyanna heard the magic words and immediately bounded over to him, leaping up and placing her paws on his thighs. He reached down and rubbed her head. "You want to come?"

I couldn't tell if that was directed at me and Spencer or just me. I shouldn't care this much, but I was really hoping that it was just me. My brain flashed to an image of the two of us, holding hands, walking around the lake, laughing at a private joke.

"I promised Luisa that I would go kayaking with her. She's never gone before, and Jason was making it sound way harder than it actually is," Spencer said, standing up now that Lilyanna had decided Lucas was more interesting. "But you two should go."

"Lilyanna, you want to go for a walk?" I asked, loudly enough that Lilyanna started to bark. "You want to go for a walk?"

Lucas pulled his shirt over his head in one swift motion. I forced myself to look away, but I could still see the bottom of his shirt riding up out of the corner of my eye. It was like now that we had hooked up, I finally realized he was attractive, and now I noticed it all the time.

He went and grabbed Lilyanna's leash from the dining room table. She followed him the whole way, her tail thwacking against every surface she passed.

"You're not really going kayaking, are you?" I asked under my breath.

Spencer grinned, lightly punching me in the

shoulder. "I am now. I have no desire to sit here and watch you slobber over Lucas. Honestly, I don't know if you or Lilyanna are slobbering more over the prospect of this walk."

"That might be the grossest thing that you've ever said," I shot back.

Her grin got even wider. "I'll let you steal that line and use it on me sometime."

This was one of the reasons that it was nice to write Regency fiction, where everyone was polite and calm to each other, and nobody made gross sexual innuendos about slobber. Or at least, my readers didn't believe that they did. "I can't wait to use it back on you."

"I look forward to the day when I can actually do that," I shot back. Well, as long as Spencer found someone whose apartment she could go back to, because we didn't have enough room in ours for anyone to spend the night,

"Let's go," Lucas said, reaching over and brushing his hand across my back. Lilyanna was on her leash now and bounding around in circles around him. He held the leash to the side and gently stepped over it, making sure to not let her get tangled up. "Have fun kayaking, Spencer. I bet you're going to be better than Jason."

She grinned and headed off into the living room, sending me a look. A *I know what you two are going to get up to* look.

"Did you finish the chapter?" Lucas asked as we walked out the door and down towards the path around the lake.

"Yeah. I'm pretty happy with it," I said. Lilyanna rubbed her face against my leg, then went off to sniff a tree. "It was worth getting crap from Spencer to get it done. At least she's giving me crap about working too much and not my pajamas any more.."

"Your pajamas?" Lucas asked, raising an eyebrow. He stepped back and let his eyes travel up and down my body. "Why?"

I shouldn't have mentioned this. "I bought them because I really needed something, and they were the only things that I could find on sale." The emergency pajama shopping had been because I had been wearing a silky pajama set that Nate had given me for Christmas the year before. I'd worn it because he had wanted me to, despite the fact that it wasn't actually comfortable.

Right after we'd broken up, I'd thrown it out along with all of the other gifts that he'd given me. And then I'd realized that I didn't have pajamas for that night, and I'd gone to WalMart and bought the first thing I could. Which happened to be a sequined pajama set with the words *Bite Me* across the butt.

Sadly, they were really, really comfortable, so I'd kept wearing them. Spencer started laughing every time she saw them. She'd still been making vampire jokes last week.

Before Lucas could press on the topic of pajama sets, his phone rang. His mouth tightened into a line as he glanced down at it. He sighed and answered the call, setting it on speaker. "Hi, Mom."

"Lucas!" His mom's voice was too cheerful. "Are you out with friends?"

He looked over at me and rolled his eyes. "Hi, Mom. And yes."

"Mason? Or the rest of your friends? Are you with Arielle? I *really* liked her," his mom said, drawing out the emphasis.

Lucas turned bright red again. "Mom, you're on speakerphone."

"Oh, hi, Arielle!" His mom's voice was even louder and more cheerful now. "I'm guessing you're there, because Mason already knows how much Lucas likes you."

"Mom." Lucas stared down at the phone, like he could will it to mute itself. "Were you calling about something?"

"Just checking in," she said, her voice dropping back to a more normal volume. "Do you want to call me back later? Enjoy your time with Arielle, okay? I love you!"

"Love you too," he said, rolling his eyes at me and hanging up the phone.

Lucas talked to his parents about me. That was a new piece of information that my brain was going to need to turn over a thousand times in the next day.

"Your mom is so cool," I said, reaching over and looping an arm around his waist.

"My mom is overbearing and embarrassing, is how I would describe it, but I'm glad you think it's cool," Lucas said, pulling me towards him.

"Trust me. I'd give a lot to have a mom like that. Or a dad like that." If Lucas told his parents I wrote novels, his mom would probably march out to the local bookstore and buy every copy. It was weird to be jealous of someone's parents, but I was.

He sighed. "My parents try to fix everything, and sometimes I just want to tell them that it's my life."

"What do you mean, your mom is overbearing?" I asked, turning towards him and changing the topic. Part of me wanted to hear the downsides so that I didn't feel so jealous any more, because I'd loved Lucas's parents when I met them.

He sighed, running a hand through his hair. "I had a really rough time with depression and anxiety in high school. I have two older brothers, and they're both really big deals."

"But you're also a big deal," I said, my hand resting on his back. "You're one of the top students in the whole computer science department. And that's not an easy department, even if Spencer claims it's just imitation physics."

Lucas snorted. "Classic. But I think that my parents are worried because I'm in a tough major. They keep telling me that it's okay if I don't get the best grades. My mom calls me to make sure that I have friends and I'm not too stressed. Sometimes I want to just tell them I'm okay and they should stop worrying."

"I get that." I rested my head against him.

His hand brushed my back again. "I get it, too. I mean, their perspective. I had a really dark time in high school, and my mom is petrified that I'll go back there. They'll do anything to make sure that I feel okay. They even bought the house so that I could have somewhere where I wouldn't get woken up by parties."

"That's a lot. But nice of them," I offered.

He looked down at me "I'm not complaining about them, to be clear. Just sometimes, I want to tell them to lay off."

"Do you think we could average my parents and your parents?"

He snorted. "No thanks. Yours just sound too awful for words. I can't stand how they make you feel."

My stomach flipped, and I stared forward. Sometimes it felt like too much, all the honesty from Lucas. He wanted to protect me from whatever was going to come. He wanted to make sure that I was okay.

I couldn't think about that right now. Our relationship, whatever it was, was crashing from fun into extremely serious.

Time for a topic change. "As soon as I get my own

health insurance, I'm going to make a therapist very happy," I replied. He wrapped a hand around my back, and I closed my eyes for a second, leaning into him.

"We can go together," he said, his fingers massaging my back. "A two for one special."

"Deal," I said, leaning into him.

Chapter 21

Of course my parents had booked me in first class. The guilt trip was already starting. Now my mom could remind me that she had spent all the money for the plane ticket, and I should be grateful.

I stared down at the free mimosa sitting in front of me, then downed it in a single gulp.

It was my dad's fiftieth birthday, so I was stuck going home for the weekend. I should have been working on the edits to the book, since I'd gotten Margaret's comments back two weeks ago. I needed to send something back soon. But nope. I'd have a weekend filled with awkward conversations and fake pity over my breakup with Nate.

The plane touched down and I grabbed a coffee as I called a car. I had had to get up at an unreasonably early hour for a college student in order to make it to my flight and to have enough of a margin of error, a Spencer term, to make it to brunch.

I climbed into the car and stuck my bag in the backseat, still cradling my coffee and giving myself the pep talk that was going to get me through today. It was twenty-four hours. Then I would be back on the way to college, and after this year, when they were still paying for credit hours, I never had to listen to them again. Just get through this one thing.

The car pulled up to my parent's house, which was decorated in true my parents style. There were floral sculptures all around the yard, and a brand new fountain had a water show going on. They'd gone full Real Housewives for this one.

I grabbed my bag out of the backseat and headed into the house, pushing open the front door.

"Arielle!" My mother clacked towards me, already wearing a white dress and heels. "You're late."

So *great to see you* would have been nice. "I came straight from the airport," I said, setting my bag down on the floor next to me.

She paused for a second, looking down at her watch and then up at me. "There's a lot to be done before people come. You wouldn't believe the trouble I've been having with the caterers." She paused and looked at me again. "You're going to change before brunch, yes?"

"No, I wasn't planning to change before brunch."

I had just gotten off a plane. I had gotten up early this morning. Relax.

"You don't have anything that's," she started, pressing her lips together, "a bit more flattering?"

Wow, okay. "Nope."

"It's the first time that you've been home in a while." She looked at me again. "I would have expected you to put in a little more effort for this."

The blood was already starting to rush into my ears. This was why I hadn't come home in months. "I've had a really busy semester at school, Mom. It's a big thing that I was able to come down here. There's so much that I have to do before my final exams."

"You know that these events are very important to our family," she said, looking up and down my outfit again.

I swallowed. I just had to get through the weekend. I wasn't going to pick a fight when I didn't have to. I was going to stay calm and get through this. "I know. That's why I'm here."

She turned and started to walk away. "I have a few things that you could borrow. Come with me."

No. I was fine with how I was dressed now. I didn't need a makeover to look exactly like my mother. "Really, Mom. I'm okay with this dress."

"Is that Arielle?" My dad's voice came from the room next door. He walked in, already dressed up in a button down and nice pants. "You arrived."

"Hi, Dad," I said, turning towards him and giving him a hug. "Happy birthday."

"We are so happy that you could come home for the weekend," he replied, releasing me from the hug. "It's so important that we can celebrate this as a family, you know?"

"Family is the most important thing in life," my mom agreed, looking over towards my dad.

"Now that I'm older, I know how important it is," my dad added. "And so we're very glad that you're here."

Something about all of this felt off. They were talking too much about family, about me being here. But maybe that was what happened when someone turned fifty - you got suddenly sentimental.

My mom glanced down at her watch and then over at my dad. "The guests will be arriving in a few minutes, if we can all go over to the dining room."

"The guests?" Of course there were going to be guests. Mom would describe it as a family brunch, and then I was going to have to sit through another talk about how the business was doing.

My parents didn't turn back, walking straight into the dining room. I stopped behind my chair in the dining room, resting my hands on the back of the chair. "Mom. Who's coming to the family brunch?"

"Happy fiftieth birthday! And what a beautifully decorated dining room you've got!"

Oh no.

I knew that voice. I'd known that voice since child-hood. That was Judith. Nate's mom.

"Mom!" I hissed under my breath. She knew that I didn't want to see Nate's family. That we had broken up. And she'd invited them to what they claimed was a small family thing?

She refused to meet my eyes and turned back towards the door.

Where Nate himself had just walked in.

My brain felt like it was going to melt down. Like I was standing at the end of a tunnel, and I wasn't really here, and my breathing was starting to get faster.

I hadn't seen him since the breakup. Not since he'd thrown away our relationship because he wanted to have fun in college. Not since I had realized that I was hiding my dreams and making myself smaller to be around him.

"Hey, Ari," he said, taking a step towards me. He was close enough that I could smell a whiff of his cologne. My heart raced. It was like all the times in high school, all the times that I had been at a football game with him, him sitting next to me, kissing my forehead.

I opened my mouth, but nothing came out.

Out of the corner of my eye, I could see my parents making eye contact with Nate's parents. "Why don't you two youngsters sit next to each other?" Judith asked, glancing over at my mom. They shot each other smiles. "I'm sure that will be far more interesting than having to listen to us the entire time."

God save me from this. I couldn't do this.

My parents hadn't believed me when I told them why. That was bad enough. But to force me to have brunch with him?

Nate took the seat next to me, nodding towards me. I pressed my lips tighter together as I sat down.

"Nate, your parents tell me that you've been taking on more and more responsibility at the business," my dad said, turning towards him. "It's impressive for someone your age."

"Just doing what I know is the right thing to do," he replied. He simpered. You weren't supposed to use those words in writing, because people thought they were overblown, but I was making an exception right now.

"You're really making the most of college," my mom said, smiling at him. Yeah. He was making the most of sleeping around and getting wasted on a Tuesday. The true college experience.

"We're so lucky to have such a motivated and wonderful son," Judith said, beaming at both me and Nate from across the table. "Don't you think so, Arielle?"

Nope. I wasn't going to engage in this conversation. I muttered something under my breath and took a long slurp of the coffee in front of me.

"So how's the new model selling?" Nate's dad

asked my dad. I stared down at my coffee, pouring more into my cup. The longer I was drinking, the less I could talk. God, there needed to be alcohol at this brunch. Not that I supported using alcohol to take the edge off, but it would be something to do with my hands.

We made it to the main course, and I stared down at the eggs on my plate. Nate got bacon and sausage and steak, and I got egg whites and avocado. Great. My mom striking another blow in favor of diet culture.

Nate leaned back in his chair and draped an arm around the back of my chair.

For a second, it was like the world stopped. Like I flew back three years in time, to how Nate would always rest his arm on my chair. Like he was showing that we were together and nothing would break us apart.

Until he did.

I closed my eyes for a second. "So how's it going up there in the cold?" he asked.

"It's not that cold." I wasn't going to agree with anything he said. I wasn't giving him an inch in this conversation.

He stuck a piece of bacon in his mouth. Asshole. "You're still living with the crazy girl? What's her name again?"

It was like he went out of his way to be an asshole. But he wasn't coming for my best friend. "Her name is Spencer. She's not crazy," not that he should be using that term in a derogatory way anyway, "and we're still roommates. We have a beautiful apartment."

Take that, you jerk. He didn't seem to notice. "I moved into a big place with a bunch of the guys. I have my own suite, though. Mom and Dad wanted to make sure that I had enough space. Don't want to spend college living in a shit room, you know?"

It wasn't a shit room. Nate had hated Spencer when he first met her, making some comments about how it was proof that most people wouldn't stay friends with their roommates after college. And he'd thought that the apartment I thought was cute was terrible. "There isn't even central air, Ari," he'd said the first time he walked in. "And how the hell would you throw a party in here?"

And I'd taken his words to heart and actually changed apartments because of it. I'd been such an idiot. I'd lost a three thousand dollar security deposit because I listened to the asshole.

I did breathing exercises under my breath. Breath in slowly, and out slowly. In slowly, and out slowly.

"Nate," my mom said, turning back towards him. "I heard that you're up for Phi Beta Kappa this year."

Wonder how much that cost him. At least whoever he was paying to give him test answers was getting their rent paid. "Of course," Nate said, leaning back and flexing in his chair. "I'm really making the most of college."

"You definitely have your priorities in order. Business is a good major," my dad said, leaning over towards Nate's dad. "You did a good job raising him."

Well, what did that say about my parents? I reached back for my coffee cup. More caffeine, less talking.

"Well, it was so lovely to see all of you," Judith said after another ten minutes of singing Nate's praises, standing up from the table. "I can't tell you how excited we are to properly celebrate tonight."

"And for both of our families to be back together again," my mom said, reaching over and clasping Judith's hand. "The way it should be."

Oh no. We weren't going there.

"I'll see you tonight, Ari," Nate said, taking a step closer to me and pressing against me in half of a hug. I stepped back, knocking over a glass of water on the table.

"I'll see you," I managed to choke out. *I never want to see you again in my life, and I hope you go somewhere and die of incurable syphilis, alone and with a shriveled dick.*

Nate's family left the house, waving back to us. Nate turned back around, flashing his eyes at me and smirking. Maybe that had been attractive one time, but now it just made my blood run cold.

My mom turned towards me. "Can't you see what a wonderful young man Nate is?"

He gave me herpes because he was sleeping around, and then I had to break up with him, and really, he's a piece of shit. "I'm going to go to my room to get ready for later," I said, turning away from my mom. I couldn't deal with hearing about stupid Nate today. I couldn't.

I reached my room, frozen in time from when I had moved out to college. There was our prom picture, my hair in the ugliest style I'd seen, wearing a giant pastel dress. I reached over and tore it down, ripping it in half. I didn't need a reminder of that time of my life. There were still photos of me and Nate on the wall, things my mom had left up. Probably on purpose.

I wanted to scream, but that wasn't going to get me anything. So instead, I reached for my phone. I started a FaceTime call.

"Hi!" Spencer yelled, answering the call. I looked behind her to see a giant robot. Damn it, she was at a tournament this morning. "Is everything okay?"

I wasn't going to ruin her morning. She needed to be focusing on whatever you did at robotics tournaments. "Just wishing you luck!" I said, trying to force my voice to be believable.

She narrowed her eyes. "Are you *sure* everything is okay?"

"Of course!" Someone yelled her name in the background, and I shook my head at her. "I'll call you later."

"Okay," she said, and I hung up before she had

the chance to protest more. God, I really needed my friends right now, but Raleigh was shadowing a surgery today and couldn't get her phone either.

Well, there was someone else that I could call. I dialed the number.

"Arielle?" Lucas's voice came through the other end. He'd picked up after two rings, sounding slightly out of breath. "Is everything okay? You made it home safely?"

"Everything sucks." God, that was an understatement. I couldn't do this. I could barely do a day with my parents, let alone Nate.

"Are you okay?" he repeated. His voice was even more urgent now.

"Not really. I mean, my parents just made me sit through an entire brunch with Nate, and they won't stop talking about what a great guy he is, and I don't want to be here any more." I caught a sob forming in my throat and let it out, then swallowed. I couldn't cry now. I wouldn't be able to stop.

Lucas swore under his breath. "That fucker."

"I just – " I paused for a second. I couldn't just unload everything on Lucas. This was my past, my problem. I wiped away a tear. "I guess I just wanted to vent."

"You should!" His voice was tenser and tenser. "Your parents are making you spend time with that asshole."

I nodded, taking a deep breath. Breathe in,

breathe out. A panic attack now would just make it worse. "I'm sorry. I didn't mean to call you in the middle of whatever you were doing."

"Arielle." This time, he used my whole name, like he was serious about this. "Please. I want you to call me when stuff like this happens. I want to know what's going on. And if you're okay." I could hear him swallow. "Are you okay? Tell me the truth, please."

It was the *please*, like he knew that I was lying. "I'm okay." Or if I wasn't okay, I was going to figure out how to be okay soon. Because I had another stupid party tonight.

In the background, I heard someone calling Lucas's name. "I should let you go," I said, suddenly feeling guilty for calling him in the middle of everything. I was asking him to fix everything with Nate and family, and I couldn't do that for myself. I couldn't demand that from him.

"Call me any time, okay?" His voice was low and tense again. "I'm here for you, Arielle. Please let me be here for you."

Chapter 22

That afternoon, I stared at myself in my childhood mirror.

My mom had picked out the dress that I was going to wear for this evening's gala, because she hadn't been satisfied with the dress that I had picked out for myself. I was in a long dress with an open back, more form fitting and sexier than my choice.

Probably because she wants you to get back together with Nate. And your practical plane dress wasn't made for seduction. I closed my eyes for a second. I could pretend that I was getting ready for a party at school, and Spencer and I were going to drink cheap tequila and go out. I was just trying on clothes for the fun of it.

My phone vibrated. *Come outside.*

That was Lucas's number. I stared at it for a second.

He must have talked to Spencer. Last time I was

home, Spencer had ordered me an ice cream cake after my parents refused to let me have dessert. She'd had it delivered, and I'd gotten to sit outside and eat all of it. It had been awesome.

I walked down the overly dramatic staircase in the middle of the house, then pushed open the front door.

Lucas was standing there, a tiny bag at his feet, sunglasses propped up in his hair. "Lucas?" I asked, my voice cracking. This couldn't be possible. This had to be a dream.

"Arielle!" He took a giant step towards me, coming over and wrapping me in his arms.

"What are you doing here?" This didn't make any sense. Lucas was here. Standing in front of me.

"I got your call," he replied, taking a step back and tucking a hand under my chin. "I couldn't stay at school knowing what your parents were making you go through."

"So you flew down here?" I asked, my hand resting on his side.

"I took the first flight that I could get." He stared down at me, reaching out a hand to brush my forehead. "God, Ari, I'm so sorry."

But you're here now. It didn't matter that I was going to have to see Nate tonight. Because I was going to be doing it with Lucas by my side. Lucas, who knew the real Arielle and was proud of everything I'd done. Who knew what I'd gone through with Nate, and flew down to Southern California for me anyway.

Things were going to be okay now.

I wrapped my arms around him and pulled him in for the tightest hug I could. *I love you* was on the tip of my tongue, but I swallowed it down. I didn't want to say it now when I was so upset. I wanted to say it when he knew I meant it.

"Your parents went all out with the decoration," he said, nodding around the house. He leaned down and picked up his bag, following me in through the front door, his hand on my back.

"If you're talking about the flowers, the ice sculpture, or the balloon arch, you should just know, this is potentially not as bad as it could have been," I replied.

"You've had more flowers than this?" He was still keeping his voice light and fun, like I wasn't freaking out a little bit about everything. His hand rested on my back as we walked.

"This is just my dad's birthday. Wait until you have to see a wedding anniversary. Those are worse." Damn it, now it sounded like I was inviting Lucas to my next family thing. I wasn't coming to another family thing, and I wasn't dragging him into it.

"Arielle?" my mom called, walking into the foyer with her phone in hand. "Did you let the caterers in?"

Oh no. I forced a smile onto my face. Lucas stepped next to me and stuck out his hand towards my mom. "Nice to meet you, Mrs. Mack. I'm Lucas Wolf."

She flicked her eyes up and down him. "The person I've been speaking to is named Vincent. Could you please tell him – "

"Mom, Lucas isn't here from the caterers." She turned straight towards me, ripping her eyes away from Lucas. One eyebrow went up. I swallowed again. "Lucas is my plus one for tonight."

His hand pressed harder into my back, letting me know he was there. My mom stared at me, her mouth opening slightly. "Your *what*?"

"He's with me." I didn't know what the right word was to describe our relationship, but that phrase felt right. Lucas had flown down here because he was with me. He was here for me.

My mom pressed her lips into a thin line. "I – "

I knew her well enough to know exactly what was going through her head. She hadn't told me that I could bring someone tonight, but she couldn't tell me no now that Lucas was here. Sucked to be her, but I didn't feel bad at all.

"It's lovely to meet you, Lucas," she finally said, forcing a smile that didn't reach her eyes. She couldn't even blame the Botox for that one. "And how do you know Arielle?"

"We go to school together," he replied. His hand was resting firmly on my back now. "We have a lot of friends in common."

"And what are you studying?" my mom asked. Of course. "What do your parents do?"

"Why does it matter?" The words were out of my mouth before I could stop them. Lucas was a thousand times the person Nate was. It wouldn't have mattered if he was studying to be a clown.

Lucas's hand pressed into my back more. *I'm here. It's okay. You don't have to fight for me.* "I'm studying computer science."

"Something useful," my mom said, glancing towards me. Of course. But at least if she was choosing to pick on my major, she wasn't talking about Nate.

Lucas looked ready to open his mouth, but I reached out and pinched his side. He didn't need to fight that battle for me. My parents were never going to understand how much I cared about English. And at this point, that was the least of my worries.

"Well, why don't you two make sure that you're ready for this afternoon?" my mom asked, her voice artificially sweet.

I nodded, taking Lucas's hand in the most obvious way that I could. "Let's go. You can come see my childhood bedroom."

As soon as we were back in my room, I slammed the door behind me.

"Has she been treating you that way all weekend?" Lucas asked, taking a step towards me and reaching out to wrap his hand in my hair. "That was awful, Arielle."

I loved the way he made my name sound. "But

you're here now," I said, sitting down on the edge of the bed. Lucas sat down next to me, wrapping his arm around me and pulling me towards him. He buried his face in my hair. I closed my eyes.

"We fly back tomorrow," he said, his voice soft in my hair. "We just have to get through tonight, and then we're going to be back to school, and you won't have to worry about any of this."

"I know." I had one night in front of me. I could do one night, especially when Lucas was here with me. "Ready for this?"

"YOU WERE NOT KIDDING that your parents were going to make this party a lot," Lucas said, bending down to say the words directly into my ear.

"Welcome to the world of Southern California car dealership owners." My dad was the most obvious and obnoxious of them, but a few of my parents' colleagues were just as bad. There was a sixty year old man here wearing gold chains, a twenty-something with a lot of plastic surgery hanging off his arm.

Lucas raised his eyebrow at a woman who was forcing her date to take pictures of her posing in the fountain. "So are you going to give me the backstory of all the people here?"

"I don't know half of them," I admitted. Or I had wanted to forget them after things went downhill with Nate. I'd cut contact with them because I was tired of having people only see me as Nate's girlfriend. *The Mack girl,* that's what I was always called. Never Arielle.

"Even better. You can make up backstories for them, and I have to guess if they're true," he said, bumping me gently with his hip. "And we know that you're good at making up stories."

I snorted. "I can promise you that no one here is a Regency lord about to face an arranged marriage"

"That's what you're working on?" he asked, taking a pig in a blanket from one of the waiters who was wandering around. I glanced up at him, and he grabbed a second one for me.

"You would be surprised how many people like the arranged marriage genre. I think it's because it says something about learning to love the one you're with," I replied.

"I can't tell if that's depressing or comforting," he replied.

"Depressing," I replied. "Imagine having to write it. You have to believe that people will be happier if someone else chooses their life for them. It's a pain to come up with something where the character has enough proactivity and motivation that you want to cheer for them, but at the same time, they're operating in this world where the main thing that defines them is their partner."

The side of Lucas's mouth twitched up into a grin. "Is this a topic that you have strong feelings on?"

"I wouldn't say that I have really strong feelings, but when you write romance, you have to think about the example that your books give. There are people who are in really bad life places, where they've never had a good role model for a healthy relationship, and they're going to pick up your romance novel because they think it's safe. And it's this wonderful opportunity to – "

"I think that you're about to tell me again why romance novels are really the most important of all literature," he said, the smile straight across his face now.

I swallowed. "I mean – "

"That's a good thing. I love it when you do that," he said, the words coming out like they were normal. "It is extremely attractive when you get passionate about something. Trust me."

I blushed and looked away, staring out over the crowds of people at the party. Lucas telling me that I was attractive was not something I was ever going to get used to. That I ever wanted to get used to, to be honest.

"Do you want another one?" he asked, nodding down towards my drink. I'd mostly finished it, and what was left was warm.

"I wouldn't mind one," I replied. I would admit that my mom knew how to pick caterers. The drinks were delicious.

"I'll grab a couple more for us," he said, nodding towards the bar.

"I'm going to run to the bathroom while you do that." The perfect moment for a bathroom trip, so I didn't have to stand here by myself feeling awkward.

He grinned at me, leaning down and giving me a kiss on the forehead before he headed off towards the table with the drinks.

"Who the fuck is that?"

I whipped around to see Nate standing next to the pool house, his arms crossed over his chest. "What are you doing here?" I asked.

"I asked you a question first," he said, his arms swinging down next to his sides. "You bring some random dude here in front of me?"

I swallowed. "That's Lucas," I said, finding my breath again. I could do it. I would tell Nate to never speak to me again, the way I'd never gotten to do. *Lucas is my boyfriend,* I started to say, but Nate cut me off.

"We're supposed to be here together, Ari." He took a step towards me. "That was the deal."

"What deal?" I took a step back involuntarily. Part of me wanted to run away. When we were dating, I would apologize and admit that I was wrong. Because Nate was right. Nate was always right.

But I wasn't that person any more. I straightened up, staring back at him. He couldn't intimidate me now.

"We're supposed to be together." His voice was rougher than I remembered, so different from the memories that I used to have.

"I'm happy," I said, swallowing again. I was happy, and he couldn't take that away from me. "And I choose what I do and who I want to be. Not you, and not my parents."

"What the hell is that supposed to mean?" Nate took another step towards me, and I stepped back.

Straight into someone. An arm wrapped around me, keeping me from losing my balance.

Lucas was standing behind me, a drink in each hand. His eyes were boring straight into Nate. "Is something the matter?" he asked, his voice low and steady, his eyes never leaving me. His jaw jumped.

"Who are you?" Nate spat out, narrowing his eyes and staring at Lucas.

"I'm Arielle's boyfriend. Lucas Wolf," Lucas said, his voice completely calm. He handed me a drink and then stuck out his hand to shake with Nate. "And you are?"

My heart was pounding. The dizziness was starting. Oh no. Lucas placed his hand behind my back and started to massage it. *It's okay. It's going to be okay.*

"Arielle's boyfriend?" Nate asked, his voice rougher. He took a step towards Lucas.

Lucas set his drink down and stepped in front of me. "You've had too much to drink, bro."

My breathing was starting to get faster. I closed my eyes. Not now. Breathe through it.

"Ari, stay with me," Lucas said, his voice low. His hand was on my back, and I focused on that. I could feel Lucas's hand on my back. It was going to be okay. It would be okay. Lucas was here.

I closed my eyes tighter. Breathe in, breathe out.

And then I opened my eyes to see Nate lunge towards Lucas.

"Nate, stop!" I screamed, splashing my drink all over him, leaning forward and trying to push him away. I wasn't going to let him hurt Lucas. Not Lucas.

Nate was strong, but he was drunk. Lucas pushed him to the side. Nate stumbled, tripping over a lounge chair and falling backwards.

Nate careened into the pool. He threw his drink forward as he fell, the glass splintering against the concrete. Droplets of water sprayed up. Everyone turned to look.

I had to get out of here. "Let's go," I said, grabbing Lucas's hand.

I pulled Lucas into the house. "I have to get out of here," I said, turning towards Lucas.

"Are you having a panic attack?" His Adam's apple jumped in his throat. His hand wrapped around me, centering me. "Are you okay?"

I took another breath. "Getting there. I really want to get out of here."

He swallowed again, his jaw jumping, then took a

deep breath. "I'll get your bag," he said, leaning down and kissing my forehead.

He started up the steps. My parents marched in, my dad's face red. "What the hell happened out there?" he demanded.

I stared at my parents. My dad's face was torn apart with anger, his cheeks red. My mom's face had tightened. "You ruined our party. And your plus one," my mom spit the words out, "pushed Nate into the pool!"

He didn't push Nate into the pool, Nate was drunk and –

Nope. I wasn't going to apologize. "I ruined your party?" I asked, taking a step towards them again. "Seriously?"

"All anyone is talking about is how you pushed Nate into the pool! How dare you do that to him?"

"How dare I do that to him?" My vision was blurring at the sides. I gulped air. "How dare you?"

"Arielle – "

"No, seriously!" I gulped air again. The words I'd choked back all day were coming up. "How dare you spend this whole weekend forcing me to be around someone I went no contact with. How dare you let our family friends be more important to you than I am."

"You know that they're our closest friends," my mom said, her voice sharp.

"And you know," I said, pointing at my dad, "that I broke up with Nate!"

"And you know how much damage control we had to do after that?" my dad roared back. "Because you were being a stupid girl?"

The room was completely silent. I could hear my breath. I could do this. I could stand up for myself.

"I'm leaving." The next words were mine. "I'm done."

"Arielle – "

I didn't turn around. I wasn't giving them the satisfaction. "Lucas?" I asked. He took a step towards me, and his hand on my back again. "It's time to go home."

Chapter 23

I snuggled into the couch in Lucas's apartment the next morning. Spencer had come over as soon as she'd heard that we were back from Southern California, skipping a robotics lecture. "This is way more important than the Mars rover," she'd declared as soon as she walked in the door. Then, turning towards me, "what in the ever living hell happened?"

I'd given her the rundown from the blowup over text as best I could. "I can't believe that your parents didn't defend you at all," she said, throwing her bag down and sitting down next to me. "They tried to put you back together with that cheater. It's completely inappropriate and out of line." She pushed the espresso I'd made towards me. "And a fountain with a water show. That's just trashy."

"My dad sells used cars. What else do you expect?" I asked, reaching for my coffee.

"You're not distracting me with your normal rant, as much as I just want to make fun of their decorations," she said. "You have to set boundaries with them, Ari. You can't spend the rest of your life having to deal with this stuff."

"My parents aren't the kind of people who respect boundaries."

"All the more reason that you need to set them," Spencer shot back.

"I know. It was the last straw. I just have to figure out how to go no contact," I said. It was tactically more difficult than I had thought. I didn't know whether to tell them or just to do it.

"Okay, you don't want advice, you want to rant," she said, reaching over and taking a drink of my espresso. "You should tell He Who Shall Not be Named – "

"Voldemort?"

"No, the other one. That if he ever shows up here, I'm going to punch him."

"He won't come up here. It's too far away from where he's getting laid at school," I replied. "But I will accept your generous offer anyway."

"The least I can do," she replied. "If you won't let me build a killer robot, I should at least get to punch the guy. And I'm just saying, it wouldn't be hard to repurpose my robot from this weekend."

"Food's here," came a voice through the doorway.

Lucas walked in, holding bags of the best bacon egg and cheese sandwiches to be found within twenty miles.

"I get to take one of these before I go, right?" Spencer asked, standing up. "I should really get back to my Mars rover lecture."

It was a sign of how much she loved me that she'd skipped that. "Bye," I called to her as she left. I tucked my legs under me on the couch and looked down at my computer. "I can't believe that I lost an entire weekend day to that nonsense."

"Are you writing today?" Lucas asked, heading towards the espresso machine. I unwrapped my egg sandwich, breathing in the smell of bacon. Take that, Mom. Lucas had even gotten me extra bacon. He was the best.

"Waiting for Margaret to get back to me with the final comments," I said, taking a giant bite of sandwich. I'd done a little bit more on the plane back from my parents', then sent it in. My draft had been late enough that I didn't want to make it any later, and I'd decided that it was better to send it in partially done.

"That must suck, the waiting." The espresso machine made a gurgling noise. I looked up at him hopefully, and he looked back towards me. "Are you telling me that you want me to give this one to you?"

"If you didn't, I wouldn't be unhappy."

"I'm going to call you out for a sloppy use of a

double negative. My professors would have been all over me for that. Don't use a double negative where you mean to use a positive."

"I'm a communications major, not a computer science major."

He grinned and set the coffee down in front of me. "And you're saying that inappropriate use of the double negative is a good communication tactic?"

I stuck out my tongue at him. He bent down and kissed me on the forehead. "Here's your coffee. I'll read between the lines and make myself another."

"Thanks," I called after him as he walked back towards the espresso machine. "Or, not no thanks."

He looked over his shoulder and rolled his eyes at me, and I stifled a giggle. I opened my computer and started to look through the rest of the homework that I had for class. After the presentation that had gone horribly awry, I didn't actually have that much left for the rest of the year.

Lucas sat down next to me, opening his own computer. I snuggled into him. He rested an arm around me and started typing.

We sat like that for a while, him doing whatever he had to do for class, me skimming an article about the future of communications in a changing world. It was not the most fascinating thing that I had ever read.

I flipped back to my email, getting ready to send Lilith a sarcastic email about our reading. There was a new email sitting right at the top of my inbox, from

Margaret. No subject. I opened it, my heart starting to pound.

Arielle, it started, not even bothering with a formal greeting,

This isn't Regency fiction. This is contemporary romance with fancy dresses. It's not Athena Brigette at all.

I don't mean that to sound too negative, because this is a much, much better book than you turned in before. I'd be happy to get this as a submission in our contemporary romance line, but that's not what you were hired to write unfortunately.

I can give you a week to redo it in Regency style, but we are running up against a tight deadline here. If you can't get this in order ASAP, I will have to cancel your contract for the Athena Brigette line. This is your official notice. Let me know if you want to talk.

Best, Margaret.

She actually put a period at the end of her name. Adding insult to injury.

"Shit." I stared at the screen. How had I screwed this up so badly? I knew how to write regency. I'd been writing for Athena Brigette for years.

"What's wrong?" Lucas asked, turning and resting his head on my shoulder. He started to read the email over my shoulder, and I pushed my computer away.

"I should have known. I thought she was going to love it, but of course I should have known better," I said, flicking my hand at the computer screen. "It's not Regency."

I needed the money from this job. I had just a

couple months left of school. And this was my plan. My lifelong plan. I was going to become a writer. I wasn't going to make a ton of money, but I was going to at least make enough to live on.

But that plan required me to know how to write. And apparently, I couldn't do that.

"Hey." Lucas's hands started massaging my shoulders. "It's one bad piece of feedback. That's all."

"She's going to fire me. And worse, she's telling me that I don't even know how to write," I said, staring down at the email.

He pulled his hands off my shoulders and started to tap on his computer. "What are you doing?" I asked, turning towards him.

"Athena Brigette does it again! I didn't think that I could like this kind of romance, but I found myself completely taken by how Lady Valencia struggles with her family and what she wants. I'm going through a lot at home, and this book was just the right thing," he read, his eyes on the computer screen.

Oh no. "Are you reading the reviews? I told you to never read the reviews!" I didn't want him to read people telling him that I wasn't a good writer, that what I did was shit.

"Have you seriously never read a review?" he asked, shaking his head. "Arielle."

"I have enough critics in my head. I don't need to hear other people criticizing me." I already had my parents and Nate.

"I mean, I get that. And there are plenty of jerks out there. But there are also tons of people who think that you're awesome," he said, one hand reaching over and resting on my leg.

I turned towards him slightly. "People don't think I'm awesome."

"Ari!" He shook his head and looked down at his computer again. "I never thought I was someone who would like romance, but oh man. I couldn't stop swooning at this one. When my mom said she read Athena Brigette, I said no way, but I loved the whole book."

I started to say something, but he held up his hand. "Another one. Maybe it sounds dumb, but Athena Brigette saved my life. This was one of the books that convinced me that I had to get out of an abusive relationship. It was like, I was reading about how women were treated four hundred years ago, and it still felt better than where I was. So Athena, if you ever read this, thank you!"

I blinked back a tear. I had always thought that romance was underappreciated, that it was the kind of genre that could change the world. But I had never thought that it was going to be my words that were going to do it for someone.

I did that.

"See?" Lucas said, his hands going back around me. "Even if you don't believe it right now, you are a writer. You can do great things."

I closed my eyes for a second, trying to blink back tears. I leaned into Lucas, breathing in the scene of his deodorant and his shampoo.

Maybe I was even stronger than I had always thought.

I swallowed. "I guess Margaret told me that I could write good contemporary romance, just not good Regency. So maybe I should just write that."

"You definitely should!" Lucas scooted next to me. "I read you the reviews. People love your writing."

Sometimes I couldn't quite believe that Lucas was real.

I got up and started walking towards the espresso machine, him following me. "It's such a big leap, though. And it's not like I've been doing a great job with the Regency lately. My sales numbers are falling, so it doesn't feel like she'd recommend me to transfer lines."

"Maybe that's because you've been trying to do the wrong thing. Maybe you've found the right thing, and you just need to trust yourself to take it," he said, his eyes meeting mine.

I stared at him. This wasn't about writing any more. This was about us.

He stared down at me for a second. The air between the two of us seemed to have become electrified.

He came closer towards me, closing the gap

between us. "Can I kiss you?" he asked, his voice lower and hoarser than before.

"Yes," I said, my voice dropping to meet him.

And then he took a step towards me, closing the rest of the gap. I stepped backwards, and he wrapped his arms around me, lifting me up and setting me down on the couch.

I leaned back on the couch, staring up at his face hovering above me. "You're perfect," he said, the breath rushing out of him. He propped himself up on the couch on his elbows, his body hovering over mine. "Do you want to keep talking about your amazing writing?"

"I think that we have better things to do," I said, my breath escaping me again. My back was already arching towards him.

"Good answer," he replied. He bent down and kissed me, his hand running around my waist under my shirt.

It felt this time like we weren't just kissing, but making a promise. That after everything we'd gone through in the past two weeks, he was telling me that he was here.

And he wasn't going to leave. That no matter whatever else happened, Lucas wasn't Nate. He was always going to be here for me. And he was going to love the real me, a romance ghostwriter with an English major and a messy apartment.

I opened my lips, and his tongue met mine. My hands tightened in his hair, and he groaned into my mouth.

Very slow, he pushed my shirt up. His finger ran along my chest and over my bra. I pressed into him, trying to get closer, wanting to feel everything.

"You are the best person I have ever met," he said, stopping as his hands brushed my inner thighs. His weight pressed into mine, and he kissed me again. "You are the best romance writer." He kissed me again. "And the funniest person." He kissed me again. "And a thoroughly average dog walker."

"Hey," I said. I grabbed his shoulder, rolling over so that I was on top of him. "Don't insult my dog walking skills."

I rested my forehead on his, and we breathed together. His hands ran back up to my sides, holding me there. I pressed my hands into his biceps, holding him under me. I pressed myself tighter against him, leaning into him and pressing my lips against his. I wanted to tell him how much I wanted him here.

He took my bottom lip in between his teeth. I started to gasp, and his tongue was in my mouth again. I dug my fingers into his biceps again.

He flipped us over again, him on top of me now. I pressed my hands under his shirt down, feeling the muscles of his chest. I pulled his shirt up slowly, and he returned the favor.

"Have I mentioned you're the best?" he murmured into my ear. "Damn it, Ari."

I wrapped a leg around him, trying to pull him closer and closer to me. I could feel him getting hard under his shorts and pressed against him harder. He groaned into my mouth, kissing me harder.

He grabbed me and pulled my other leg, drawing it closer and closer towards him. His hand slid between my legs, and I groaned. He knew the right spot, exactly where to go.

I couldn't think of anything but Lucas now. Just Lucas, and his hands all over me, his weight all over me, him all over me.

His fingers circled around the opening, and I groaned again. "Fuck, yeah," he breathed into my ear.

"Do you want to get a condom?" I asked, not recognizing my own voice. It was too soft for this, not demanding enough.

"Do you want me to?" he asked, his fingers still down there. I closed my eyes against the rush coming over me.

"Yes," I breathed back. He rolled off me, kissing me on the forehead before heading into the bedroom.

This was the best. That I could lie here and wait for him to come back without thinking of anything else. That there wasn't a feeling of needing to think through things, just knowing that things were going to be good. Because it was the two of us, and nothing else mattered.

He was back a moment later, sliding on top of me again, kissing me as though we hadn't seen each other in months, not just seconds.

He started to press into me, and I pushed back into him. I could feel it in my entire body, in every part of me. That there was nothing else in the world I could want.

"You're my person," I said, my eyes meeting his.

"You'll always be my person," he replied, his voice raw.

I pushed the hair out of his forehead that was there, smeared with sweat. I touched his chin, the corner of his mouth, wanting to take in every part of this moment.

He slid out and back into me, bit by bit, wanting to hold the moment as long as I did. His hand slid down between my legs again, and I could feel the heat building.

I kissed him, pressing closer to him. He sighed, and the noise was enough that my muscles pulled together, making me feel him even more strongly.

I closed my eyes as the heat rolled over me. It was an explosion, the first sunshine after a storm, everything. I let out a groan, tilting my head back and losing myself in the moment.

"Hey," Lucas said a second later, his hands

running up my face. He'd rolled off, lying next to me, his hands still around me.

"Hey," I said back, staring back at him. He smiled at me, his hands brushing the hair out of my face.

This was everything.

Chapter 24

I was already in bed when the phone rang.

"Hello? Spencer?" I called, rolling over and reaching for the phone on my nightstand.

"What's wrong?" asked a deep voice next to me. Not Spencer. Lucas.

"My phone," I said, and he made a noise and rolled over.

I pushed my hand around the darkness. The phone kept ringing. I grabbed it and swiped to answer, rolling out of bed. "Hello?"

I stood up and walked out of the bedroom, closing the door behind me. I wasn't going to wake Lucas up if this was Spencer butt dialing me in the middle of the night. But it was a weird time for her to call.

Nothing but noise on the other end. "Hello?" I said again.

"Ari?"

I froze. The voice on the other end wasn't Spencer. "Nate?" Oh god, it couldn't be my parents, it couldn't be that something had happened to them, that there was something terribly wrong, that –

"What's going on?" I swallowed. Tell me, get it over with, I wanted to say. I can be on a plane in the morning if they're in the hospital.

"I wanted to talk to you." His voice was gravely, barely audible over the background noise.

"At two in the morning?" I swallowed again, feeling acid rising up in my throat.

"Yeah. I just wanted to hear your voice."

"Well, you've heard my voice, so I'm going to hang up now and go back to bed." *And block your number*, I mentally added.

"Don't hang up." His voice was panicky. Oh no. Nate wasn't supposed to panic. He was an asshole. I heard his breath through the phone, and I closed my eyes.

Hang up, screamed a voice in the back of my head. *Hang up. Go back to sleep. You owe the asshole nothing.*

But then, the part of my brain that remembered being in love with him clicked on. *Stay. Listen. You have enough years together to owe him that. And anyway, what if it is about your parents?*

"I miss you, Ari." His voice dropped. "I don't know why you left me."

Because you were cheating on me with anyone

who'd sleep with you? "Shut up," I said, my heart starting to pound. "I don't want to talk to you."

"But I love you," he said.

It suddenly felt still in the room. Like everything that I had been thinking vanished for a second. I closed my eyes against the headache coming on. "What?"

"I love you, Arielle." His voice was louder now. "I've always loved you, you know that. And I know that I made mistakes, and that you don't want to see me any more, but I'm telling you, I'm a different man. I'm going to come back into your life, it's going to be the Nate and Ari you always wanted."

"Stop," I said, closing my eyes. We had broken up. I was happy about it. But the dizziness was starting, and I had to shut my eyes tighter.

"But I need you!"

Oh no. The anger was coming now. Good. This was what I wanted. Righteous, earth scorching anger. "You don't need me, Nate. You don't want me. You made that clear. And I'm not coming back to you, so just shut up!"

"You're holding one little mistake over me and ruining the rest of my life with it!"

"One little mistake?" He cheated and gave me an STD. That wasn't one mistake. That was a lifestyle.

"We're in college, Arielle. What were you expecting?" The words sounded more like he was spitting them out.

I had just expected that he could be faithful while we went to college. But even that had been too much for him. "Clearly too much!"

"Get over it and stop ruining my life then!"

"Ruining *your* life?" He'd been the one who'd cheated and moved on. He'd left me with the consequences. Emotionally and physically.

"My parents won't give me the business if you don't get back together with me."

Silence.

"What?" His parents and my parents were really going to pull that? Fine. Let him face consequences for once in his life.

"You know how much money that's worth, Arielle?" He was almost spitting the words. "If you don't get it together, we're both going to be broke."

"You called me and told me that you loved me because our parents are holding your trust fund back?" It wasn't even me. It was so Nate could keep partying with his parent's money.

"Your parents think you're being an immature bitch," he shot back. "You – "

There were tears running down my face now. I didn't know if they were from anger or sadness at this point. But I was going to guess anger. Frustration.

"Your parents tell me everything. They think you're a failure." His voice was a sneer. "And so do I! I'm going to write romance novels, I'm so artsy, oooooh."

It's good but it's not what I asked for. You failed the assign-ment. We need to find a new ghostwriter.

"Don't contact me ever again, Nate." I swallowed, closing my eyes. The world was starting to spin around me. "We're done."

"We're – "

"I'm hanging up."

And this time, it took all of my strength. But I did it.

There was silence in the room after I hung up.

The room started to spin. The dizziness was coming.

I had to get out of here. I had to be by myself for a little bit. I had to process this. My breathing was speeding up again. No. I wasn't going to think about this yet.

I grabbed a sweatshirt from beside the door. I had to find my shoes. I had to get out of here.

"Arielle?" Behind me, Lucas came wandering out of the bedroom. He rubbed his eyes. "What are you doing?"

I tried to open my mouth, but nothing came out. The dizziness was worse. The panic attack was coming. "I need to go."

"What are you talking about?" He rubbed his eyes again, slowly waking up. "It's the middle of the night."

I couldn't talk about this. I needed to be alone. I needed to breathe again. "I have to go." I reached for my shoes, sticking my feet in. I pulled the sweatshirt over my head.

Lucas rubbed his eyes. "Ari — "

"Don't call me that!" Not right now. Not when I still hate Nate's voice ringing in my ears. I pulled a sweatshirt down. "I have to go. I need to be alone right now."

And before he could say anything before he could stop me, I pushed open the front door and ran out onto the street.

Chapter 25

"What the hell is going on?"

There was light streaming through my window. That was the first thing I noticed.

The second was Spencer standing over me, arms crossed, her phone in her hand.

"Spence?" I looked up at her, then down at my feet, still stuck into a pair of shoes. Oh shit. The memories from last night were starting to come back. Walking home in the middle of the night, opening the apartment, crawling into bed.

"Lucas has called me six times to see if you're okay," she said, crossing her arms tighter over her chest. "What on earth happened?"

I closed my eyes again. "I'm okay."

"You are not okay. You are lying in your clothes in your bed. Your boyfriend has called me six – " she looked down at her phone "now seven times to make sure you're safe. You've been crying. Again, what the hell is going on?"

That was all it took. Everything came rushing back over me, and I started crying.

Somehow, over the next half hour, I managed to explain the whole story to Spencer. How Nate had called me, how I'd snapped at Lucas, how everything felt terrible and overwhelming.

It had just been a panic attack. I knew that. Or I knew that now.

But I'd run out of the apartment. After Lucas had done everything for me, I'd shut him out.

I'd broken things. I'd let the past throw me back, again, and I'd ruined things with a person I loved.

"We have to get out of town," Spencer said finally, pulling me in for a hug. "Let's give you time to process."

"But I – " I had broken things again. I ruined something good and beautiful. I'd found something wonderful and destroyed it.

"I'm going to tell Lucas that you're okay," she said, standing up and fetching me another cup of tea. "And you're going to take a shower, and then we're going on a road trip. You need a few hours to process, and then we're going to fix things, okay?"

I nodded, forcing myself out of bed and heading towards the shower. Spencer was not going to take arguments this morning.

"She's okay," I heard Spencer's voice on the

phone as I got out of the shower and started to dry off. "I mean, she's safe. But I'll let her tell you how she's feeling when she's ready."

There was a voice on the other end. It had to be Lucas. God, I had screwed it up so badly. I pushed him away and ran out of the apartment. "Don't worry. I've got it. She's with me, okay?"

I turned on the hairdryer and missed the rest of the conversation. Probably better, because I wasn't sure what else I was going to be able to hear and not fall apart again. I had pushed Lucas away. The person who would have done anything for me, and I'd shut him out when I needed him most.

"Ready?" Spencer asked as I walked out of the bathroom, fresh clothes on. There were tote bags of snacks and things in front of her. I looked down at the bags, and she clapped her hands at me. "We're going on a road trip. And we're going to stop along the road and we're going to have fun, Ari. And when you're ready, you can handle the shit that your family has dumped on your lap. But not until you're ready. I don't care how far we have to drive."

I was going to start crying again. Everything from the last couple weeks was hitting again all at once. And this time, it was hitting with the knowledge that I was the one who had messed it all up.

Like she knew it, she walked over to me and wrapped me in a hug. "This is what best friends are for, Ari. I'm here for you."

She was right. I needed to get out. I nodded and followed her outside. "Are we sure that Lazzie is going to be able to handle this trip?" I asked as we walked out to the sidewalk. It was what we always said, and maybe if I said what I always said, it would make things hurt less. I could joke through it.

"Lazzie knows this is an emergency, and will absolutely pull through. And if not, I brought an extra roll of duct tape," Spencer replied, opening the driver's door. It creaked. "Come on, let's go."

We started the drive out of town, the landscape around us starting to become more tree covered. "You want to pick some music?" she asked, nodding down towards her phone. It was attached to the car via a mess of cables.

"Anything?" Spencer was too picky about music to let me get away with that.

"Come on. We're on a road trip. There's a road trip playlist in there," she said. We'd done this before, when Spencer had had a particularly bad breakup. And we'd driven for hours, ignoring Lazzie complaining. I scrolled through her phone, looking for the playlist.

After two hours of blasting the music as loudly as the old speakers could go, Spencer pulled over next to a lake. "I'm thinking it's time for a picnic and a snack," she said.

"Isn't a snack included in a picnic?" I asked,

turning towards her from where I'd been staring out the window.

"No. The picnic is the part where we sit next to the lake and talk and make fun of things and laugh about the fact that you picked the ugliest sweatshirt to steal last night. The snack is where I eat food because I'm hungry," she replied, turning down the music so she didn't have to yell.

I grabbed another of the bags and walked with her down to the lake. We were the only people there, and I could hear the birds chirping around us.

I sat down on the ground, spreading one of the picnic blankets around us. I closed my eyes for a second, leaning back into the sun. "Do you think I'm a failure?"

"What?" Spencer's head turned towards me.

I took a deep breath. "Nate told me last night that I was a failure. And I guess that I sometimes feel like I'm not good enough, or that I've taken on too much. Like can I really be one of the few people who makes a living writing?"

Spencer turned towards me, this time with her whole body. "You are listening to Voldemort's opinions about anything?"

She had a point there. She passed me a can of seltzer, which I cracked open. I reached into the bag and pulled out a pack of grapes. "You know," she said, "making money from writing isn't the only reason that you should do it. I mean, you love it, and maybe you can't make a living full time from it, but maybe you just have to know that and try."

I nodded. She was still silent next to me, as though she knew that I needed the time to think about what I was going to say. I swallowed. "My editor is about to fire me. Margaret told me that my last book was a lot better than my other ones, but she'd have to fire me if I couldn't turn in a Regency novel."

"But she told you it was much better. Maybe it's that you don't have to just write Regency. If the best thing you've written so far isn't Regency, maybe it's time to try something new," Spencer said.

But this is the Athena Brigette line! screamed a voice in the back of my head. This was the highest profile opportunity that I'd ever had. There weren't many opportunities that were going to be better.

But Spencer had a point. I didn't just have to be Athena Brigette. I could get my start writing Regency, but I could try something else, too.

Writing for Athena had been great. I'd proven to myself that I could be a writer. But maybe it was time for the next challenge. I didn't have to do the same thing. I wasn't the Arielle who I'd been so many years ago, and I didn't have to be.

"I've been thinking about it," I admitted. "It just feels like so much to ask, especially when I haven't been doing well."

"You don't have to apologize for wanting to do something new, you know. You can be the person who writes Regency and then something else." She shrugged, reaching into the bag again. "People change."

People could change. I'd proven that.

Well, mostly. I glanced over at Spencer. "Do you mind if I do something really quickly?"

I walked back towards the car, unlocking my phone and dialing a number that I should have blocked long ago. The phone rang, and the answering machine clicked on. "It's Nate. Leave a message, yo."

I closed my eyes for a second. His voice sounded so familiar, so trusted. But that was my past now. "Hi Nate," I said, swallowing. "It's Arielle. Ari Mack." As though he wasn't going to know who I was. "So the conversation we had last night — that was really shitty of you. It's officially, officially over between us. You're an asshole. I'm going to block your number. Don't contact me again." I paused. "Oh, and make sure to get tested."

I hung up the phone, staring down at it for a second.

And then, before I could think of anything else, I went to my contacts and blocked his number.

Around me, the world was still quiet. I waited for a second, for some sign from the universe that I had just done something big and bold and brave. But nothing.

And then Spencer's voice, "I've got ice cream!"

Chapter 26

"Spencer. This door is literally about to fall off the hinges," I said, looking down at my door, which was vibrating alarmingly.

She looked over at me. "We have a mile until we're back at the apartment. I believe in Lazzie."

"I believe in Lazzie too, but I think that my door may literally fall off." I wasn't sure that Spencer was quite grasping the situation.

"I have duct tape in one of those bags if it gets really bad, but otherwise, maybe just send the door good vibes," she replied, bobbing her head to the music.

"I don't think that good vibes are an approved car repair strategy." For someone who was so smart in so many ways, Spencer sometimes lacked common sense.

"Good vibes are going to need to be a car strategy,

because I don't want to have to stop and get the duct tape out," she replied.

I held my breath as we turned onto our street. As Spencer had promised, I was starting to feel a whole lot more relaxed after the road trip. I'd called Nate and told him it was the end. And I had a plan now.

Well, I was more relaxed about everything except the impending car disaster. Lazzie made a thudding noise that sounded like it could have been our muffler falling off.

"Come on," Spencer chanted under her breath as we drove up in front of the apartment. The car groaned and came to a stop in front of the house.

"Good car," I said, leaning forward and patting the dashboard. "You did good."

"You did well," Spencer corrected. She grinned at me. "I love correcting the English major's grammar. Have I mentioned how much joy it brings me?"

I rolled my eyes at her, opening the door and grabbing some of the bags out of the trunk. "Seems like the kind of thing that would bring you joy. Physics majors have to take it where they can get it."

"Good reply," she said, shaking her head. She grabbed a few bags and followed me up towards the apartment.

"Arielle."

The voice stopped both me and Spencer in our tracks. Standing outside our apartment building was my mother, her arms crossed over her chest.

Spencer glanced from me back to my mom and back. "Um – "

"What are you doing here?" My mom wasn't the kind of person to just drop in to say hi.

"We need to have a discussion about what happened at our party," she said, crossing her arms over her chest.

"We can have this conversation inside," I said finally, nodding towards the apartment.

Spencer tensed behind me, and I glanced over at her. "Killer robot," she mouthed towards me. I could feel my shoulders loosen a tiny bit. At least I had Spencer here.

"This is your apartment?" My mom looked around the room, her eyes narrowing.

"It is," I said. Part of me wanted to run around and start to clean things up, to make things look more presentable. But I forced myself to stop. I wasn't going to apologize for what things looked like. This was my apartment, and I was comfortable here. It wasn't my mom's apartment.

"You could have – "

I cut her off. "I don't want something else. This is where I live, and I like it. And that's what's important to me."

She stared at me for a second. "What is wrong with you, Arielle? We raised you better than this."

"Better than what?" I asked.

"This!" She swept her hand around the apartment, at the robot pieces scattered around the carpet. "We raised you better than the person who would bring someone home who was so rude to Nate, and then just vanishes after the party, and don't get me started on the way you – "

I closed my eyes for a second. My heart was starting to beat faster, but this time, it didn't feel like a panic attack. It just felt like anger.

"You know what?" I said. "I changed my mind. This is my apartment, Mom. I pay the rent. And that means that I can decide who I want in my space." I saw Spencer out of the corner of my eye, fist pumping and urging me on. "And I don't want you in my space if you're just here to insult me."

She stared at me, her mouth opening into a fish shape. "But – "

"I'm setting boundaries." The words came tumbling out. "If you and Dad want to talk to me about my life, you have to first accept that I'm doing it on my terms now. I'm not going to stand here and let you make me feel bad for wanting something different in life."

"I flew up here," my mom started, her face pulled tight, "and I will not have you speak to me that way. You are a shame on the family."

"I want you to leave now," I said, swallowing and staring back at her. I was saying it. I was finally saying it.

"You can't – "

"I think you heard her." Spencer took a step towards us, swinging a roll of duct tape around her arm. "If you don't get out of my apartment, I'm calling the cops."

My mom stared at me and then went back to Spencer. "You – "

"Are not on the lease and have no legal right to be here." Spencer stared my mom directly in the eyes, then slowly reached her hand into her pocket and pulled out her phone. "You have thirty seconds. I'll start counting."

My mom's mouth dropped open. "Any questions?" Spencer asked, smiling sweetly at my mom. "Because if not, the countdown starts now."

And for the first time in her life, my mom backed down.

"We'll discuss this later," she said, turning and pointing towards me.

No. I had boundaries now. "We won't," I said, finding my voice again. "When you're ready to engage on my terms, you can call me."

My mom slammed the door behind her as she left. It was the first time in her life that she'd slammed a door. Firsts for both of us.

"You did it!" Spencer screamed, launching herself at me and wrapping me in a hug. "You did it!"

It still hadn't quite processed that I had done what I had waited for years to do. that I had finally told my parents what I wanted, and maybe it had taken

Spencer, but I thought that they might have finally listened.

I sat down on the couch, the adrenaline running through me. "Holy shit, Spencer. I did it."

"You did it!" She danced around me, waving her hands in the air. "I am so proud of you, Ari."

I shook my head. "I can't believe it." For so long, I'd thought that I just had to deal with my parents. I'd finally stood up to them.

"I told you you could," she said, still grinning at me. "You're a badass, Arielle Mack."

I sunk back into the couch. There was just one thing left to do. "Can you help me with one more thing?"

"STILL NO SIGN OF HIM," Spencer said, staring through the binoculars we'd stolen from Raleigh. We were in Lazzie's front seat, staring out the windshield. "Are you sure you can't just go wait on the front porch?"

"Have you ever read a romance novel?" I asked, shaking my head. "This is a grand gesture."

"The what?" she asked, lowering the binoculars for a second.

"Okay. At the end of every romance novel, there's a thing called the grand gesture. Where the person who's fallen in love does something totally over the top to show the other person they care Like, it usually involves kissing in the rain and a lot of running," I said, peering out the window.

"I would have worn better shoes if you'd told me there was running involved," Spencer said, looking down at her sandals.

"Not for you. For me," I said. That was the whole point of the grand gesture. You needed to prove how much you needed the other person. You would do cardio for them.

"You're in luck, because it's starting to rain," she said, looking up at the sky above us.

Oh damn it. The universe was going for irony today.

My plan had been to intercept Lucas on his run. We'd gone by his house, but there was no sign of him. And I couldn't sit there until he got back. I had to go out, and I had to tell him how I felt. I had to open up again and let him in.

It was like I was so close. I knew what I wanted. And I wasn't going to let him get away from me.

"There!" Spencer said, pointing in the distance. The shape was still far off, but I knew how it was. That was Lucas.

I jumped out of the car and started running towards him. Above me, it started to sprinkle.

Of course it was going to rain. It was a grand gesture. What would a grand gesture be without some rain?

"Lucas!" I shouted, running towards him.

"Ari?" He sprinted towards me, then stopped. "Are you okay?"

"Yeah," I said, breathing heavily. I hadn't run in a long time, and all of my muscles were letting me know that. "I have to talk to you."

"Now?" He looked at me and shook his head, still breathing heavily from his sprint. "Are you okay?"

I was bent over, catching my breath. I took another gulp of air and stood up straight, looking him in the eyes as much as I could. "I have to apologize."

"For what?" he asked, stepping towards me.

"For running out on you." I closed my eyes for a second. "Nate called, and I got upset, and I ran away because I didn't know how to deal with all my feelings."

"Ari. You scared me so much." He ran a hand through his hair, his eyes still on me. "I had no idea what was wrong, and you were just gone. You ran out of the house in the middle of the night."

"I know. And I shouldn't have done that. I should have talked to you. I should have known that you would be supportive." I swallowed. "I'm so sorry, Lucas. I need to let you in, and I promise you, I can do better than I did."

He took a step towards me, and I closed my eyes. "And I guess – " I continued, not sure if my voice was going to keep going or not, "I've fallen for you. Hard. I love you, Lucas Wolf."

He stared at me for a second. "I – "

"You don't – "

"I love you too, Arielle Mack." He wrapped his arms around me and lifted me into a hug. He was sweaty from the run, and it was pouring rain now, and there was no place that I would rather be.

I had found my home.

Chapter 27

"I'm just saying, nobody looks cute in a graduation cap," Raleigh said, adjusting the cap for the hundredth time.

"Disagree," Mason said, reaching over and giving her a kiss on the forehead.

Spencer rolled her eyes at me, and I grinned back. Something about the end of college had been making Mason extra touchy, and it straddled the boundary between cute and nauseating. "I could have offered to make you one of my cap throwers," Spencer said, holding hers up so that we could all admire the tiny spring she'd put inside of it.

"I don't want my cap flying up into the stratosphere when I throw it, but thanks," Raleigh said, adjusting a piece of her hair.

"It won't actually go into the stratosphere. Too much drag," Spencer replied.

"Spencer, you know that you're going to knock someone out with that hat when it finally falls back down," Lucas said, coming up beside me and wrapping his arm around my waist.

I turned and smiled up at him. "Do you think that Spencer cares about that? She's just trying to have the highest flying graduation cap of all time."

"You're all just jealous that you didn't take majors that allow you to catapult a graduation cap properly," Spencer replied, sticking out her tongue at me.

"This is why you're going to graduate school in *Boston*," I replied. Spencer had gotten into a very, very good school for her Ph.D., but she had stopped saying the name of the school to avoid being mansplained to about school rankings. I'd settled for saying *Boston* as loudly and slowly as possible.

"She made the wrong choice. I'm going to have sunshine all the time," Raleigh shot back. "I'm telling you, if you call USC up, they might still let you in."

"As much as I want to go to grad school in the same place as you and Mason, I can't pass this up," Spencer said. "Plus, you might get bored of all that sunshine and start begging for a Boston winter soon."

I snorted. "I'm looking forward to all of the trash talk from you two."

"We'll see who you visit more," Raleigh replied.

Lucas's arm tightened around my waist. "We are not answering that question right now. Not when

Spencer has a graduation cap that functions as a projectile missile."

"We'll see. Margaret told me that I might have to do some traveling for work this upcoming year," I replied.

It turned out that getting fired from the Athena Brigette line was the best thing for my career. Margaret had been pretty honest when she'd finally told me. "You've got a lot of potential, but you need practice, and you're not getting it in Regency."

It had sucked for a few days, but then I'd called her back and asked her how she thought I could grow. She asked me if I'd ever considered starting as an editor. I hadn't even thought about it until she mentioned it, because it seemed impossible to break into the field.

She'd made me an offer to join as one of her assistants. I was going to be reading romance and editing it for a living. I still thought that I wanted to go back to writing someday, but I was really excited to start. And who knew? Maybe I'd love being an editor even more than being a writer.

"Hi, all of you!" Lucas's mom yelled from a hundred feet away, waving as though she was flagging down a plane. "We're getting seats! Wave to us when you walk, okay?"

I waved back, and Lucas shook his head. "They will never stop embarrassing me."

"And that's totally okay," I replied. I hadn't invited my parents to graduation, and they hadn't asked.

Maybe someday we'd start talking again and find our way back to a normal relationship. But they were going to have to accept who I was before that. Until then, we'd settle for a text telling me happy graduation.

The music started, and I looked around at my friend, my chosen family. "We ready for this?" Lucas asked, his hand resting on my side.

I looked up at him, then towards the doors leading into the stadium and then off campus, onto our new lives. I squeezed his hand. "Yeah, we are."

Clarke spent her twenties figuring out her life - with stints as a professional tree counter, an amateur reality show producer, and an English teacher abroad. Today, she focuses on writing stories about other people going through that journey. In her spare time, she hunts for the best iced coffee and ice cream, avoids parallel parking, and reads an excessive number of books. She lives in New York City.

www.ingramcontent.com/pod-product-compliance
Lightning Source LLC
Chambersburg PA
CBHW061605190726
48288CB00007B/2185